POCKETFUL OF TIME

Tom Burton

Hope you enjoy these stories!

T. Burton

First published in Great Britain in 2021

Copyright © Tom Burton 2021

The right of Tom Burton to be identified as the author of this work has been asserted by him in accordance with the Copyright, Designs and Patents Act 1988.

Typeset in Garamond

ISBN: 979-8-72649-590-3

CONTENTS

BELIEVER

'This is our patch!'

'We were 'ere first, you bastards!'

I shove away from my desk, limp to the window and peer into the damp street below. Two jeering crowds of rival gangs squaring off, around seven or eight either side. I watch the posturing, the drunken bragging, the catcalls and swearing of 'these're *our* streets', and 'shog off, you cunts!'

Always the same on a Friday night. Leather flasks of wine drained, stale grudges oozing out. Bored young men spilling out of taverns and roaming the streets, hunting for excitement. The usual buildup; spitting at feet, thumbing of noses,

1

hands on daggers. Any petty quarrel will do for idle apprentices hungry for a brawl. Soon the clubs and knives come out.

Just what this place needs: another glorious chance for the French to jeer at us. Many's the time I've walked through the French enclave and seen a mother scold her child: 'Stop that grizzling, or I'll fetch an Englishman.' English armies laid waste to the French countryside they marched through, robbing and raping for forty miles either side of their baggage train. They torched crops in the fields, burned down farmsteads with the families still inside. They butchered priests and hung them naked in marketplaces, ransacked churches and fed their cooking fires with precious gilded books. They torched the corpses of the dead before their families' eyes, without ceremony or a single prayer, as one might the carcasses of diseased cattle. We're bloodthirsty hooligans from the cradle, always spoiling for a fight.

And now the turf war's right outside my front door. Terrific. With a sigh I slip on my boots and shoulder my medical bag, then head downstairs to an anxious household clustered in the hallway. Bess is in her nightgown, brown hair down and bleary-eyed by the window. 'What's this about, Mark?' Liz and Joan cling together in their nightshifts, forlorn and whimpering until Meg appears and shepherds them away. Our little dog Grace slinks around my ankles, whining. Edward waits by the door, fully dressed and alert, cudgel at his belt. 'Here if you need me.'

I shake my head. 'Go back to bed. Just some drunks larking about. I'll deal with it.'

Don't get involved. Close the shutters. Get some bloody sleep.

The meaty thud of an ugly punch. More heckling from the rabble outside.

'Beat 'is arse, Richie!'

'Fuck 'im up, Ben!'

Ugh. I square my shoulders and open the door. Peacekeeping's a nightmare.

Puddles everywhere. The sour reek of a nearby piss alley. I keep to the shadows and scan the scene. The carpenters' gaffer and a young bricklayer are circling, swiping at each other with wooden staves. The occasional thump and grunt of pain. Both idiots are injured; the gaffer's free arm hangs limp, his sleeve bloody. An ugly bruise across the bricklayer's cheek. Lucky his

3

eye wasn't damaged. Definitely battered ribs judging by how they're shuffling awkwardly, stiff like they're hurting bad. I join the ring with the timber boys. 'What's it about, lads?'

A crooked yellow grin. 'Nuffink. Brick boys gotta fight wood boys.'

'Like Lancaster and York?'

'Like tha'.'

'Ever heard of Towton? Over twenty thousand Englishmen died there.'

The lad gapes at me. 'Who were they fighting?'

'Each other.'

Palm Sunday, 1461. The armies of two kings smashing together in a raging snowstorm. King Edward the winner, if you could even call him that. The river choked with corpses, its banks black with bloody slush. Untold thousands crawled away through the freezing mud: blinded, broken, mangled for life.

Enough of this horseshit.

I wade in, rip the staff from the gaffer's hands and send the other clattering onto the cobbles. The bricklayer staggers away nursing a bruised arm. I shove them both and they tumble over backwards: two crumbly Englishmen, chalky teeth, snappable bones. The onlookers veer away, like startled magpies rising from carrion.

'That's *enough*.' My best surgeon voice; the calm, icy growl that made even glowering sergeants flinch and listen up.

Everyone stops. And stares. Not surprising. I'm the wrong side of forty, a thickset slab-faced bruiser with muscle already running to fat. The puffy eyes, mussed hair and ink-stained fingers don't help either. But I make it crystal clear who's in charge through my rocksteady posture and stern scowl, the same look that cowed fellow soldiers and made even snarling dogs cringe back in shame. Use every trick taken to heart to become the most important presence there. It works a treat.

'Everyone sit down.' Most of them do immediately; one of the more cocky brick boys edges forward looking mutinous, until I turn and crush him with a glare. 'James Weaver, sit your sorry arse *down*.' James hesitates, then sits. 'How's your father?' I ask lightly, knowing that will deflate the others. James mumbles a shamefaced reply as I seat the two glowering fighters down safely away from each other. The gaffer's boy – and god, he *is* just a boy, can't be more than thirteen or fourteen – winces as I ease off his leather jerkin.

'Name?' I bark, cleanly gliding my knife up his sodden shirtsleeve.

'Richard,' the boy grinds out. 'Ow! Watch the shirt.'

'I don't *care* about the damn shirt,' I growl as I clean the puckered flesh around his wound. 'I *do* care if you never get to use your arm again because this wasn't stitched right. Hold still.' Richard hisses as the needle presses through, then looks away, jaw clenched.

'Everyone hear me?' I ask. A ripple of grunts from the knot of onlookers, huddled in on themselves like timid browbeaten mice. Victors of Agincourt? Proud warriors of Albion? Their forefathers would be weeping in their graves. Good thing the French aren't here to gloat. I draw the thread through and continue sewing.

'No fighting in the street anymore, lads. I don't care what about. *No fighting.*' I bite off the excess thread, wrap Richard's arm in a bandage and turn to fix the bricklayer's cheek. His cut is shallow, the bruising making it look far worse than it actually is. Only needs a damp rag to clean up. Having to do this by guttering

6

torchlight doesn't bother me; I've done this by moonlight, starlight and in no light.

'Right lads, we're going to sort this out like I did in Italy. Despite the bad blood between you, I'll have none of it on my carpet. Inside.'

I limp upstairs; they trickle after me in unsure dribs and drabs, crowding the doorway until I find the faded street map I'm looking for. 'Let's sit down and talk like civilised people, not the jabbering apes you seem to think you are.' Most frown in confusion as I unroll it across the floor, but some seem to get it.

'I want two friends whom you trust to tell the truth of the matter. From both sides.' Four boys are pushed forward. 'Names?'

They introduce themselves with shamefaced mumblings; Richard – grimacing slightly as his stitches tug – and his opponent Benjamin, a soft-spoken hulk who introduces himself as Jacob, and Francis, a lean lad with spiky straw-blond hair. I make the four shake hands, which they do with far more grace than I expected. I hand Richard a charcoal stub and Benjamin a paintbrush of whitewash and get them to draw the current boundaries on the map. They cross. The disputed territory extends from the baker two streets away, and onward to the blacksmith three streets further south on Tanner's Lane. I choose a red paint the shade of fresh blood and get to work.

'I'm marking neutral areas,' I say. 'I don't care who you run with. Where there's red on the map it doesn't matter.' I outline red around my house and the English House of merchants, the priory chapel where choirboys sing, the butcher's, the baker's, the marketplace square.

It takes them another ten minutes to draw out boundaries that they all finally agree upon. I keep the final painted copy and date it. Any further disputes are to come through my doorstep first before descending into open violence. They shuffle out into the street, but Benjamin dawdles behind, lingering on the doorstep.

'Doc,' he murmurs, and I blink away the flashes of sweltering heat and hissing arrows and my friends screaming *Doc, we need you!* 'What did you mean, like in Italy?'

'Goodnight, Ben,' is all I say, and wait for him to leave before locking up after him. I slump against the door with a heavy sigh. Such petty excuses again – over a girl, of course, the dented pride, the jeering sneers – why is it always the petty things that start fights? A father's good name dragged through the mud – understandable. A sister's virgin maidenhood besmirched – fair enough. But scrapping over a pretty lass they both ogled like starving dogs? Bloody hell.

What we need is something that unites people, pulls warring factions together and works for everyone. It's over a century since Agincourt, yet Englishmen are still feared throughout Europe as brawlers, looters, rapists and thieves. This needs to change, and soon. Reprimanding their rowdy whelps on Antwerp's chilly streets just won't cut it anymore.

Keep your head down. Mind your own business. And don't make waves. That's what you remember in Antwerp. That's what my mother drummed into me at the London quayside before waving me up the gangplank, smiling through her tears. You're an Englishman, Mark, so mind your manners. Keep your nose clean. And don't make trouble.

For Antwerp is not a free city, though its overlords allow free men in it. The Emperor's black double-headed eagle soars over the walls; from Lübeck to Trieste, Bruges and Vienna,

Europe cowers beneath the vast darkness of his sable wings. Charles has a sticky web stretching across the continent, a web of money and terror ensnaring merchants and lawyers, judges and monarchs alike.

A grey windless day, a sea of unbroken cloud above. I shrink back against the wall as another armed patrol tramps along the wharf, pike butts tapping the cobbles. The Emperor's troopers are everywhere; I saw them hauling a merchant out of his home opposite the Jackdaw tavern only this morning, their pleading captive wide-eyed and dishevelled as his wife sagged in the doorway, their children clinging to her skirts.

The curses reach me first: 'Get a bloody move on!', 'Satan's sweaty balls, lend a hand here, Percy!' I glimpse them at the end of the wharf, away from the bustling stalls and buzzing chatter of the Sunday market crowd. 'Lift your end, Tom, fuckin' hell!'

I smile. Fellow countrymen, of course; nobody swears quite like the English.

In the shadow of the Steen's looming ramparts, three young merchants struggle with their heavy bales. A ragged mongrel watches them from the gutter, head tilted quizzically.

They try heaving the awkward baggage onto a nearby pushcart, but their overflowing armfuls droop like bundles of sodden reeds; bulky samples of woollen cloth flop onto the cobbles. A port officer stamps up shouting about paperwork, arguing, getting in their faces. His sharp Flemish words stabbing, nicking, like a knifepoint.

I toss away my apple core and sidle closer, like any lounging Lowland idler. The customs clerk is still berating them. Behind his back I hold up six fingers – a decent bribe. The three merchants nod. 'Please,' murmurs one in halting Flemish, 'could you relieve me of these marks? I find them a real hassle. Here. Please take some.' His palm opens, gold gleams; suddenly the clerk is all smiles. As he strolls away richer, whistling, they gather around me with grateful grins. 'Come with us.'

Behind us the mongrel yawns, cocks a leg against a barrel then trots away along the wharf.

The three Englishmen haul the cart through the quiet streets as I trail behind them. Before long we reach Wool Street, the English House's twin facades looming before us. I hang back; a nest of troublemakers, these folk, if you believe the rumours floating through the streets. Best stay well clear of it.

But no: they lead me onward past those familiar crow-stepped gables, those roof tiles the shade of blood. Turn a corner. A hundred yards down Weaver Lane, we halt at another grand house – three floors of arched windows, its single gabled roof crowned with honey-brown shingles.

They turn to me on the threshold. 'Come in! Get yourself warm.'

I glance back up the street, thinking of Bess bent over her knitting and Grace curled up by the fireplace, her paws twitching as she chases dream alleycats. 'I can't, I've got places to be –'

'Nonsense!' The nearest – clean-shaven with cropped brown hair – beckons me in, smiling. 'You helped us out of a tight spot. Stay for lunch, at least?'

Can't hurt, surely . . .

'All right.' I shrug and follow them indoors.

The smell of garlic, cinnamon and cloves washes over me. Black-robed aldermen brush past on their way outside, arguing over the finer points of Luther. Giggling overhead; a blonde girl clatters downstairs chasing her yapping terrier. I hear the cook before I even see him: some clumsy little toe-rag wishes he'd never been born. 'Told you once, told you twice, laddie,' bellows a deep voice, 'use that mortar for garlic again and I'll knock out your brains meself, grind 'em into paste and feed 'em to the watchdogs!'

We go inside. 'Inky fingers out!' roars the pink-faced cook, flapping his hands at us. Then, 'Ah, Master Avery.' He doffs his cap to the grinning young man. 'Beg pardon, sirs, but you see I had Harry Wyllis down here from his account books, poking around the storeroom wanting to weigh things. Then Master Hawhurst crashing in: "Cranton, we're expecting some guildsmen for dinner later, what sort of cakes do Flemish like?" Christ almighty.' He mops his brow with a meaty paw.

Avery swipes a handful of raisins. 'What's for supper, then? How's that fish going?'

'Bloody disaster, Tom,' Cranton groans. 'Just a yellow and white mess – looked like someone's spewed it up. Got mutton instead. Soup's nearly ready.' He nods towards the bubbling stockpot; Avery lifts the lid to sniff the brown slop, like an elderly dowager admiring a fragrant rose garden.

The cook looms over me, glaring down. 'And who's this, Tom?'

'A friend.' Avery pats my shoulder. 'Mark Morton. He's with me. Helped us down at the docks earlier.'

A dangerous pause, then Cranton's face broadens into a crooked grin. He claps a heavy hand on my shoulder; it's like being thumped with an axe. 'Pleasure to meet you, sir!'

In the dining hall, we stand waiting until an old man in a long black gown totters in, followed by two others. You could swap any elder for his companions: hollow-chested, phlegmy coughs, long straggly beards, watery eyes. After a long bout of grunted negotiation, the three sniffling greybeards shuffle to their seats. 'Masters Reed, Warwick and Parris,' Tom whispers to me. 'Bible scholars.'

The servants enter bearing several dishes – leathery mutton cutlets smothered in a gritty brown gravy like Thames mud. Warwick's trembling bony hand knocks his goblet; spilled wine blots his sleeve as he bleats in irritation. The blonde girl giggles from her corner chair, flicking spoonfuls of mashed potato about while a nursemaid fusses over her.

'Alice seems very excitable tonight,' Master Parris croaks, frowning down the table. 'I trust her diet has not been too rich?'

Thomas Avery smirks down at his plate of half-chewed gristle. 'No worries about that,' he mutters. Sniggers ripple around the table as Percy kicks his ankle, grinning. Even Master Poyntz raises a hand to hide his smile.

The lady of the house clatters in, a heaped tray of food under one arm. Anna's hair is tucked under a linen cap and her sleeves are rolled up. 'Oh, *Anna*,' Poyntz laughs, reaching out to her. 'You look like a baker's wife.'

She rolls her eyes and smacks his shoulder fondly. 'You mind your manners, potboy.'

'How's our guest faring?'

She snorts. Swipes another roll from the bread basket. 'Toiling away, as usual. Blunting his quills. Ripping out his hair.' She heaves a tetchy sigh, scowls up at the ceiling as her voice rises to a nasal squawk. '"Oh please, Miss Anna, would you mind awfully fetching more spare quills?" I'll just pluck another five dozen geese we've got laying about, shall I? Glory be!'

We wince in commiseration as she clatters

about, bemoaning the piggish selfishness of men everywhere. Eventually armed with sufficient bread, she sweeps out again, calling to the waiting servants: 'Bring in dessert! More wine for Master Warwick, Cranston! And fetch extra candles; we'll be needing them upstairs.'

I raise an eyebrow at Poyntz, who blushes. 'We have a, ah . . . very *particular* houseguest lodging with us. Works long hours and, well . . . his needs *are* rather demanding. Burned through our entire winter stock of spare parchment in under a week.'

I smile as I picture a hidden upstairs room stinking of tallow and ink, seeped in old chicken dinners. Some harassed lowly clerk scribbling furiously at his desk, wailing as the candles gutter low and the light dims around him. 'Writing his life's masterpiece, is he?'

Poyntz huffs a laugh. 'You could say that.' He winks. Taps his nose.

After lunch, we each drift our separate ways. I wander through the quiet galleries as the dog snuffles around my ankles and whines for head scratches.

Voices. Loud voices raised in argument. Ahead

of me. I tread softly down a gloomy corridor to a closed door.

'. . . more than three thousand copies shipped from Worms,' Poyntz is saying. 'Dover's being watched, but Hastings and Portsmouth are still viable, and Monmouth's fleet's sending plenty over –'

'For Christ's sake, Tom,' someone else interrupts, 'No ship's fully watertight, you know that as well as I. There's, what, some four thousand Englishmen in this city?'

'Five.'

'And who's to say they're *all* pure-hearted, hmm? Not lead astray by easy gold? No, *listen* –' he raises his voice as others groan, '– just hear me out. The Emperor's coffers are far deeper than ours, we don't know how many spies More's already slipped into Antwerp –'

'But we have *faith*, George,' Poyntz mutters, 'and besides, with the cardinal away in France –'

'– with Wolsey away, More and Gardiner now have their hands free to pursue us, to brand us heretics, to leave our families shunned and penniless. You really want to crawl out your hole *now* and sail over to England?' A bitter, derisive laugh. 'At least Wolsey protects us.'

Poyntz snorts in disbelief. 'Wolsey? Wolsey burns Bibles.'

'Thomas More will burn men. And then this Morton fellow . . .'

I press closer to the door, listening hard as George continues, 'He just blew in on the wind only this morning! How do we know we can trust –'

Enough of this. I raise a fist and knock. All talk ceases. A long deathly hush.

'Who is it?' George calls.

'Only me,' I answer. 'I was just passing and, well, someone said my name?'

'Shit,' someone mutters.

Footsteps approaching. The door creaks open, and a stern face glares out the narrow crack.

'Help you?' he growls. I've been told to fuck off and die with more warmth and good humour.

'For pity's sake, George, show him in,' Poyntz calls. George hesitates, then grimaces and lets me inside.

A wintery sun casts the oak-panelled room into sharp relief, ravines of shadow and cold floods of light from the narrow windows. A half-open door near the end of the room. Seven strangers stare at me from around a table as

Poyntz introduces them: 'Gentlemen, this is Mark Morton. Mark, here is Stephen Vaughan, John Hawhurst, George you've already met . . .'

I take an empty seat as Poyntz addresses the gathering. 'More bad news, I'm afraid: Master Radcliffe was seized yesterday. They uncovered a spare copy by his printing press and arrested him on the spot. He's rotting in Vilvoorde now, most likely.'

Shudders ripple around the table. We lapse into glum silence, each imagining the poor wretch's terrible fate. A key fumbled frantically into a lock, an ancient rusty deadbolt rammed home. Heavy boots thundering upstairs. The sergeant barking orders to his men. A heavy oaken door bursting inwards with a splintering crash. Armoured troopers flooding inside with halberds, axes and swords. Radcliffe dragged away while his tearful wife begs and pleads in vain. His children's shrill screams ringing in his ears.

'So what's next?' George mutters.

'We lie low for now. There's still six more printers close by that we've used before.'

'And what about More?' someone asks.

Now Vaughan shakes his head. 'Still hunting

heretics back home. But he's far more occupied with being Chancellor now. According to Avery, Cromwell thinks –'

'Oh, that butcher's dog!' George scoffs. 'Cromwell's just a lowborn ruffian – whatever can *he* know?'

'He has the cardinal's ear and eyes in More's household,' Vaughan replies sternly. 'He knows far more than you, I'd wager.'

George turns away with a growl of frustration. 'If Tyndale were here, he'd say –'

'Say what?'

A deathly hush; everyone is staring towards the back door, where a tall figure has appeared in the shadows, a cloth-wrapped bundle in his hand. He moves forward into the light.

With a loud groan of wood the others scrape back their chairs and stand up with one accord. Remove their hats.

'Ah, gentlemen,' Poyntz blushes, smiling towards the newcomer, 'may I have the honour to introduce . . . Master William Tyndale?'

The others murmur in awed greeting as he glides among them, warm kindness radiating off him like Jesus among his disciples. A far cry from the haggard, stooped elderly scholar I'd been expecting. Instead he looks to be in his late thirties, still in the prime of manhood. True, his thick mop of curly brown hair is already streaked with grey, his forehead creased with worry lines. A weary smile around at his guests, rather careworn and tired. Perhaps a slight pallor to his face from long tedious days shut indoors. But otherwise a solidly capable man in good health.

Suddenly we are face to face. 'And this is the brave man who helped at the docks, hm?' He shakes my hand, beaming. 'Thank you, Mark!'

We seat ourselves as he smiles around. 'Now, Master Berwyck has said he's printed the final ten sheets. Just the binding left to dry, then we'll have two dozen more copies finished.' He lays the parcel on the table. It's just small enough to fit into a pocket. Anyone's pocket, perhaps. His. Mine.

Unease shivers through me. Is that package really what I think it is?

George is frowning too. 'That's *it*, is it?'

Tyndale's smile flickers. 'Of course.'

George nods, clearly seething inwardly. 'Marvellous. That's *great*, William. That's worth all the worry and dread, that is.'

Poyntz stirs, but Tyndale turns towards him,

raising a cautious hand.

'Peace, Tom,' he growls, voice edged with steel. 'I know what I'm about.' He turns back to George. 'Don't *ever* presume I have it easy.'

George folds his arms, scowling. 'You're shut up safely indoors all day, you don't understand –'

Tyndale scoffs. 'I'm a wanted man charged with heresy. What *don't* I understand?' He gazes around the room, eyes agleam with emotion. 'Every time I pick up this pen, I *know* there are thousands of people who will hate me for it. Even now, even *here*, I feel it. The stares. The judgement. And there's *nothing* I can ever do to change that.'

I glance around the hushed table; a few men are frowning at their boots, blushing with shame. Tyndale's voice hardens, firm and resolute. 'Yet I'm *still here*. Still fighting. Just look at me! No armies. No titles. No noble lineage or ancient bloodline. I'm just a writer. The only power I have is that I believe we. Can do. *Better*. I can't demand that people step up, but I *won't* let them down!' He rests a hand on the wrapped Bible. 'People have burned for this book. Bled for it. Died for it. And I won't let *anyone* tell me I can't fight for it too. Not after what everyone else suffered before me.'

A ringing silence falls. George opens his mouth as if to argue, but then Poyntz is on his feet, glaring around. 'That's quite enough argument for now. *Good day*, everyone.' He turns to me. 'Mark, can you stay behind?'

With a creak of chair legs the others straighten up and funnel out the door. Poyntz watches them leave, then grimaces at me. 'Well, *that* could've gone better.'

Tyndale huffs in amusement.

A sudden knock at the door. Poyntz stirs. Tyndale looks up and nods. I realise that these two men know – and trust – each other so deeply that much of their communication passes unspoken.

Thomas Avery peers around the door. His face is pale. 'Sirs? It's happening right now. The Italian marketplace.'

The crowd jostles us as we steer through the crush of bodies, our faces hooded. A tide of Flemish voices wash over us; we might be deep in the Italian district, but here the crowd are all locals. Poyntz, Avery and myself the only Englishmen amid a sea of pale Flemish faces.

Tyndale dares not venture outside, stray from his safe haven. Far too dangerous.

A sunny afternoon of brilliant bone-chilling cold, the wind hissing off the Scheldt like a knife blade on the cheeks. Excitement fizzes through the air. The crowd is large and boisterous, growing ever larger, drawn by the clamour. It becomes an impassable wall of flesh as we near the open square, then we see: a towering pyre of firewood.

Crowned by a wooden post.

Faint hoots of 'Traitors!' and 'Heretics!' reach us. Murmurs seep through the crowd; townsfolk chatter to their neighbours. The jeers grow louder, a venomous wave of hateful hissing. Behind us, a woman in a white muslin cap hoists up her daughter for a better glimpse. 'Up here, sweetheart. Pay attention. You remember this well.' Her friends murmur approval.

'It'll do her good,' a fat man chortles over my shoulder, 'so she always goes to Mass hereafter and obeys her priest.' The food stalls have been wheeled back against the surrounding buildings to make more room. Still the crowd thickens. Some pray aloud. Others munch pies.

Chains clanking. 'Make way!' calls an officer.

'Make way for the city!'

First come the Flemish aldermen wearing gold chains, in doublets of crimson satin and gold-fringed robes of emerald green. Then a smirking monk waddling like a fat grey rat, cross clutched in his pink paws. As he passes the commoners doff their hats and kneel, heads bowed.

'Here come the sinners!' yells a man.

When the sorry procession finally shuffles into view the people rise, hoot and catcall. Four shackled wretches in penitential smocks shuffle along barefoot, prodded by spearbutts. Three haggard men with faggots of wood lashed to their backs, their ankle manacles rattling. Each clasps a leather-bound book against his chest. And an old woman, wizened and stooped. Her scraggly grey hair is torn out in patches. Papers proclaiming her heresy are pinned all over her, front and back, her hessian shift rimmed with muck. Spectators behind me snigger 'Look at her, the wicked old crone. Seventy years old and steeped in sin.'

This is a public spectacle, meant to shame and belittle. A public humiliation. The men are paraded twice around the jeering marketplace, forced to unwrap their dry faggots of kindling and fuel the towering pyre. Menaced by spearpoints, they hobble forward and toss their Bibles onto the firewood. A triumphant cheer from the crowd as each book flops down, pages fluttering like a dove with a broken wing. The three cowed penitents step back, kneel on the cold hard cobbles as the monk harangues them.

Let it end, I silently pray. Please God, let it be over soon.

But no: a drunken chant ripples through the packed crowd, soon echoed from a hundred throats: *Chain her up! Chain her up!* Troopers surround and seize the old woman, who barely struggles. They frogmarch her forward, away from her three companions.

Towards the waiting pyre.

Chain her up! Chain her up!

'Not much meat on her,' the fat man mutters in bored Flemish. 'Won't take long unless the wind changes.' The troopers drag her forward, hoist her atop the bonfire and bind her to the stake with chains.

'What's her crime, Mama?' asks the girl on her mother's shoulders.

'She thinks God on the altar is but a piece of bread.'

The girl giggles. 'What, bread like the nice baker bakes?'

Her mother squeezes her hand. 'Yes, darling, just like that. She's a Lollar.'

'Lollard,' scoffs the fat man. 'Get it right.'

The mother raises her voice. 'Let this girl through! Let her see the wicked hag sizzle!' Others gladly make way, pushing them forward alongside us, murmuring encouragements; how pious it will be to let a child witness a burning! I meet Poyntz's bleak eyes, look past him. Only strangers around us.

Where is Thomas Avery?

The priest waddles up, bellowing prayers. He drones on how the pain of earthly fire is but a mother's gentle caress, a blissful feather touch compared to the agony of Hellfire.

The monk preaches for ten long minutes but he may as well be pissing in the wind. Somehow, impossibly, the condemned woman has rallied, drawing upon some hidden reserve of inner strength; she still has the gall to spit his own words back at him, snarling that she has remained God's devoted servant since eight years old, a true Christian maid ever since her baptism, and that he himself is no Christian. 'For what

Christian' she sneers, English voice dripping with scorn, 'would dare seduce pilgrims with shrines and Masses whilst robbing them blind, or fondle another boy's bollocks in his abbey bed? Thief! Fornicator!' The crowd groans.

The monk shakes his head at his defiant enemy. He calls out to the condemned woman. 'Recant your heresy!' he implores her. 'Return to the Holy Church! Save your soul! Repent!'

She glares back at him with utter contempt, lean and withered, broken but unbowed. Every inch a queen among cockroaches. Her lips move silently, mouthing prayers. 'Look at her,' our neighbours snigger. 'She's begging Satan to save her. Stupid old crone.' The troopers bank up fresh bales of hay around her.

'Will she burn, Mama?' asks the child, eager for a show.

Her mother tickles her feet, making her squirm and squeal. 'Aye, Jennete. As all godless heathens deserve. Good view, this; last time I was right at the back.'

The monk raises a hand, and the crowd falls obediently silent. He gazes out over his hushed flock, begins droning a Latin sermon. *Miserere mei, Deus, secundum magnam misericordiam tuam. Et secundum multitudinem miserationum tuarum –*

'In the beginning . . . was the Word.'

Gasps ripple through the crowd. A penitent brother has risen to his feet, swaying but standing tall, head high and proud, eyes shining. 'And the Word was with God. And . . . and the Word *was* God.' His voice trembles, but rings out like a clarion call. 'The same was in the beginning with God.' He raises a shaking arm toward his chained sister in Christ, who smiles back through her tears. 'All things were made by it and without it . . . was made . . . nothing that was made.'

The monk gapes at him, aghast in disbelief. A buzz of outrage swells through the front ranks as he continues: 'In it was life' (a fishwife screeches: 'Hang him! Hang the heretic!') 'and the life was the Light of men.' ('Make him sizzle!' bellows a street vendor.) Several troopers close in upon him. His cheeks are wet with tears. 'And as for the Emperor, I refuse him and denounce him utterly' (now he raises his voice above the uproar) 'as God's worst enemy . . . and ANTICHRIST!'

Crack! He crumples to the ground, face a

mask of blood. A scowling trooper lowers his armoured fist, kicks him in the belly. He convulses, groaning, but then his hoarse voice roars from the cobblestones, spitting venom: 'Emperor Charles! I curse you! The Holy Ghost curses you. God Himself curses your name. May you die a thousand deaths. (Much wailing, gibbering, gnashing of teeth) May your feet swell up and burst. May your rotting gizzards strangle you.' Amid jeers and booing the troopers hastily haul him up and drag him away. Within moments they're swallowed in the depths of the crowd.

The prisoner bows her head. Two troopers step forward, lower their lighted torches to the pyre beneath her feet. A drum begins to beat. *Boom doom boom doom boom.* The monk backs away, still chanting in Latin . . .

And then we all see it: the first curl of smoke.

The mother fills her lungs and howls, a hallooing demon shriek. Her daughter waves her fists and echoes her wild cry. The crowd seethes and surges forward, catcalling and whistling and stamping. 'Hag! Witch! Hellspawn! To the devil with her!' The troopers bar their way with staves and roar in deep voices: 'Back! Back! Get back!' The mad multitude shrieks and eddies back, then washes forward again like an onrushing tide, stamping feet, shaking fists. We stand fast in the heaving swarm of bodies, jostled by hungry-eyed townsfolk baying for blood. All around I see humans, but no humanity. Just a ravenous horde of starving beasts, drooling for their pound of meat. *Boom doom boom.* Eddies of smoke hide the view and onlookers wave it aside, coughing.

'Smell her!' the fat man bellows. 'Smell the rotten old sow! Look how she's cooking!'

'Shame on you!' someone snarls nearby. An English voice. Heads turn, and the fat man rounds on his neighbours, bristling for a fight. But blank faces everywhere, nobody knows who spoke, yet could it perhaps be Thomas Avery? The chained woman raises her eyes to Heaven, shaking with grief.

'Poor soul,' Poyntz murmurs.

When the heat reaches her she draws up her bare blistered feet. She's moaning now, twisting in her chain, feebly shrinking from the hungry tongues of fire. But the kindling crackles merrily, ravenous flames clawing ever upward, and soon she is forced to hang her legs down into the blaze. The vile reek of human flesh washes over us. Sizzling. Scorching.

31

The mother presses forward, and it's as if the lid has been pulled off some dark writhing nightmare, her face a hideous twisted mask of derangement and fury and utter viciousness: her serene gentle beauty cracks; her eyes glitter with malice and she screams, crazed and hysterical, utterly certain in her blind righteousness, '*She deserves it!*'

I lower my gaze and turn away, sickened, but Poyntz seizes my arm in a vicelike grip. 'Watch,' he growls, eyes glistening with tears. 'Don't look away. See her depart this world. We owe her that much.'

The smoke swirls aside. The woman sags against the wooden stake as the faggots around her begin to crackle, fiery cinders whirling about her. Her two penitent brothers gaze mournfully into the flames, witnessing her searing agony. My stomach curls with nausea, but I force myself to hold fast, dry-eyed. If they can forbear to watch their sister in Christ suffer, watch her burn and shrivel and die for God's word, I can too. I will watch, and witness everything. What meagre dignity I can offer this lady in her final moments of torment. The sullen pounding drum rolls on ceaselessly, *boom doom boom*.

A gust of wind sends the flames sheeting around her, licking along her legs. Above the roaring inferno, I hear her scream. 'Yah, *now* she believes in the saints!' our neighbours jeer. 'Too late, grandma! Burn in Hell!' Beside me, there's no longer any trace of warm kindness or compassion in the mother's face; only seething hatred, pure and hard and cold.

The fat man yawns. Others munch yeast buns or prattle amongst themselves, the ghastly spectacle already forgotten amid everyday banalities.

'Hope it's sunny tomorrow.'

'God, I need a piss.'

'Just feel these silk sleeves Jan bought me! Feel the lining, Hendrik!'

'Nice pie, this. Anyone want some?'

At long last the woman falls silent, hanging limp and unresisting; her legs are charred shrivelled stumps, and her upper torso begins to burn. The mob is cheering now. Laughter. Drunken singing. The drum pounds *boom doom boom*. And above it all, the foul stench of burnt meat. Like any fat rasher of bacon sizzling in the pan.

'Serves her right,' sniggers the fat man, idly

scratching his balls. Suddenly he's sprawling forward, shoved hard in the back. 'Watch yourself!' people curse as he lurches into them. In the jostling confusion one man clouts his neighbour, spilling his beer. Gets a fist in his eye. The girl shrieks as her mother sweeps her away to safety. A burly marshal wades into the brawl, jabbing about with his hefty club. 'Break it up, there! Break it up!'

The fat man staggers upright, pawing at his slashed belt. 'Where's my money?' He lurches at his neighbours, fists flailing and teeth bared. 'Come out, you whoreson dog! Which of you fuckers stole my coin purse, huh?' They cringe backward like skittish young foals.

The marshal saunters up, club smacking into his palm. 'Causing trouble, sir? What's your problem?'

The fat man rounds on him, spitting with impotent fury. 'Some bastard's robbed me!' A burst of laughter. A ribald joke about falling; big man, someone sniggers, not big everywhere. More titters. The fat man storms away through the packed crowd, livid with rage.

'Cranky old tosspot,' the marshal sneers.

The pyre is fully ablaze now, a solid sheet of

swirling fire. Nothing but a shrunken contorted shape in the flames, her mouth agape in a silent scream. At a signal, the executioners reach into the inferno with long iron poles, unhook the roasting torso from its blackened chain and pitch it into the fire below. It vanishes with a roar from the frontmost spectators, a rushing spurt of flame; and then she is gone. Nothing more but sludgy ash and charred bones, fat bubbling amid the embers.

Boom.

Doom.

The drum falls silent.

Poyntz bows his head, crosses himself. 'It's over. Go with God, sister.'

The velvet-coated aldermen slowly drift away, flanked by steel-clad troopers. The monk waddles off, clutching his cross and smirking. The commoners begin to disperse their separate ways, chattering, laughing, tossing down gnawed pie crusts and licking gravy from their fingers. Some drunken wretches are swaying with linked arms, a clumsy eight-legged beast, hallooing as if at a dogfight. Others wander off in a vacant trance, their faces grey with ash.

Thomas Avery melts out of the throng and

35

·rejoins us, looking as if he might spew on his boots. Perhaps he already has. Poyntz squeezes his shoulder. 'That wasn't you earlier?'

Avery shrugs modestly. 'Nah. Some other idiot, perhaps. Far braver than me.' The crowd is thinning; at the apple stall Avery draws me aside, glances around, then drops a fat purse into my hand. It clinks heavy with coins. 'Present for you, sir.' A shy, blooming smile. He looks towards where the fat Antwerpian had stomped off. 'From someone who didn't need it.'

Poyntz gazes back at the smoking wreckage, then wraps an arm around Avery's shoulders. 'Well done, lad.' He holds my gaze. 'You wanted to know what we were fighting.' He looks back sadly at the pall of human ash hanging over the rooftops. 'Now you know.'

Back at Poyntz's house: 'He said that?' Tyndale gasps, eyes brimming with tears. 'All of it?'

'Every word.' Poyntz lays a comforting hand on his shoulder.

Tyndale groans like a trapped animal, passes a hand over his face. 'And that brave woman,' he glances between us. 'She . . . she didn't suffer?'

Poyntz and I stiffen. 'No,' he lies. 'Her pain

36

was brief, Will. She's in a far better world than this.'

Tyndale's face hardens, and he nods, suddenly all business. 'All right, then. Let's see, I can . . . I can send word to Master Berwyck, have him print out two dozen more –'

'Christ!' Poyntz collapses into a chair, scrubs a hand through his hair. 'If they *ever* discover you sheltering here –'

'They'll what? Burn me?' Tyndale's mouth twists into a wry smile. 'Heard *that* before. What else is new, Tom?'

'Don't be so glib! This is your *life* we're talking about –'

Tyndale slams a fist down on the table. 'I owe it to them! What kind of coward would I be if I didn't honour their sacrifices?' He eases back in his seat, fingers drumming the leather-bound Bible. 'To all those brave souls who need this book, who crave it, who *deserve* it –'

Poyntz gives a strangled snarl of exasperation and lurches away from the table, fuming. 'The Emperor's agents are lurking everywhere, Will! Don't you get it? They're guarding all the doors and holding all the keys –'

'Which means that sooner or later, *someone* is

37

going to have to fight them,' Tyndale counters.

Poyntz's hand curls into a fist. 'And then, what . . . you're just going to sail over there, walk to Paul's Cross, start handing out Bibles to Londoners and hope for the best? If they catch you, they will *burn* you, man! If they haul you before a tribunal, what then?'

Tyndale shrugs. 'Then I'll say what I must before my last judgement: that the Eucharist is only bread, we have no need of penance and Purgatory is a church invention ungrounded in scripture –'

Poyntz rounds on him, incredulous. 'Jesu! Do you even hear yourself?'

Tyndale laughs softly, his eyes gentle. 'Oh, Tom . . . how many times will you ever learn the greatest lesson of all . . .'

Poyntz bristles. 'Which *is*?'

'It's not. About. *Me*.'

With a heavy groan Poyntz slumps into a chair. Buries his face in his hands.

No one speaks. After a long while, Tyndale reaches over and gently squeezes Poyntz's arm. Poyntz looks up, eyes bleak with dismay. 'I can't watch you die, Will,' he croaks.

And something softens in Tyndale's face, in

his broad shoulders, in the firm set of his jaw. Something thaws.

In a sudden flash of clarity I see it: these two men are even closer than brothers. For years now they must have worked together, united towards a common cause; Tyndale doggedly pursuing it with single-minded purpose, Poyntz terrified for his friend's life, every day glancing over his shoulder.

'I cannot unbelieve what I believe, dear friend,' Tyndale sighs, rubbing Poyntz's back. 'I wrote this book for all Englishmen to read, and I cannot unwrite it. I cannot unlive my life. I'm sorry, Tom, but . . . I just *can't*.' He takes a deep breath. Marshals himself.

A sudden lump in my throat. He believes in us, I realise. Tyndale may be the saddest, loneliest man in Europe, hounded from house to house, but he is still a great believer in people. Their innate goodness. He puts his faith in them. Here he is welcomed and sheltered by a family who need him and love him for it, and Tyndale is very much a man who needs to be needed. In return for their trust, he will give them everything he is, and everything he still has left. Until his last dying breath.

By God, the strength of this man.

'Never give up trying, do you?' I ask.

'*Never*.' Tyndale's face is pale, but his eyes gleam with determination. 'My defence is up here,' he taps his forehead, 'and here,' he places a hand over his heart, 'where it will stay safe from them.'

'*Why*?' I grit out. 'Why can't they ever face the truth?'

'Because they've been raised from the cradle to obey the Holy Church, to blindly follow the Pope. You must understand, Mark – most of these people simply aren't ready to have their minds opened to God's word. Many of them are so inured, so hopelessly dependent on the current system, that they will fight to the death to protect it.' Tyndale's jaw tightens. 'And until we can reach them all, these people still remain a part of that system. They will uphold it. They will defend it. And that makes them our enemies.'

My heart sinks. 'But they'll never stop hunting you. Stokesley. Gardiner. More.'

'I know.' Tyndale's eyes are creased with weariness. 'They think if you let people read God's word for themselves then Christendom will fall apart. No more justice, no more governments.'

I gape at him. 'They believe that?'

'That we need the constraint of blissful ignorance? Yes.' He sighs. 'I have offered them God's true word for their flocks, I pray with all my heart that someday they'll see how they are misled.' He sighs. 'But they're proud men, and their pride blinds them from all that is gracious and good.' There is sadness in his voice as if tinged with grief, and yet he speaks firmly, steadfast and resolute. 'Their task is to kill me. Mine is to stay alive. It's my role and my God-given duty for England.' He spreads his arms. 'All I own is the very ground I stand on, and that ground remains William Tyndale's. If they want it, they will have to come take it from me. I won't yield it without a fight.'

The door creaks open. Poyntz tenses and half-rises from his seat, but Tyndale grips his arm. The blonde girl, Alice, toddles inside and makes a wobbly beeline for Tyndale, her arms raised for a cuddle. With a fond smile, the scholar scoops her up and hugs her close. 'Hello, dumpling.'

'Miss Anna told me to rescue you,' she mumbles drowsily into his shoulder, arms curled around his neck.

'Did she now?' Tyndale rocks her gently. 'That's sweet of her.' Alice's head droops and she tumbles into a doze, her crown of golden curls nestled beneath his chin.

The door opens wider; new faces peer in, pale ovals in the candlelight. Thomas Avery, Anna Poyntz, even Stephen Vaughan.

Tyndale chuckles and beckons them in, careful not to jostle Alice from slumber. 'Come on in! Gang's all here, I see. No rest for the wicked.' They gather around him with shy smiles.

'We were worried about you,' Anna murmurs, 'we heard shouting.'

Tyndale pats her hand. 'All fixed now.'

Avery frowns at the cloth-wrapped bundle. 'Is everything ready?'

Poyntz nods. 'Ready as it'll ever be.'

Vaughan sighs heavily. 'We'll need to remain discreet, remember. More's men are watching the Channel ports.'

A shrug from Tyndale. 'They always are. But once the Bibles reach the Steelyard, they'll be safe there.'

Vaughan frowns. 'With Germans?'

Tyndale rolls his eyes. '*Yes*, Stephen, with the Germans. Stokesley locks up Lutherans by the

42

dozen; if this book gives them their chance of payback, they'll keep it safe for us.'

'Still a long journey.'

'Relax. More's agents won't find them.'

'But they'll still try.'

'Let them try,' Poyntz mutters darkly. I watch them all edge closer around Tyndale, closing ranks protectively: a fine English household, young and old alike united in common cause. All for a simple book.

Tyndale pats it fondly, a faint smile tugging at his mouth. Suddenly he pushes it across the table. Towards me.

I stare back, frozen with shock. 'What?'

He gazes steadily at me. Nods towards the book. 'Just . . . have a read of it, all right? Just for tonight, that's all. Then you can bring it back early tomorrow. No harm done.'

I shake my head. 'I can't. You know I shouldn't. This is crazy!' What if the Emperor's troopers come knocking tomorrow? Discover the book under my roof? Disaster for my family. Prison and certain death for me. No second chances. It's far too dangerous.

'They're offering a thousand-mark reward for anyone who turns me in.' Tyndale's stern brown eyes bore into mine. 'Anyone who discovers an illegal Bible, well . . . that's a hundred marks, right there. Easy money.'

Anna leans in, appalled. 'Why burden him, William?' she hisses, glancing at me.

Alice squirms and burbles softly, but doesn't waken. Tyndale rocks her gently. 'Because anyone who shelters a heretic but doesn't report them faces a slow burning at the stake.' He holds my gaze, unwavering and resolute. 'You saw what happened out there today. You've seen me here, and you know this house. But you support our cause. So you're now one of us.' He holds out a hand. 'Welcome aboard, Mark.'

I lie awake, gazing up at our bedroom ceiling as the slumbering household settles around us. Bess snores beside me, but I can't drift off; prickling doubts churn through my mind. The leather-bound book still lies unopened on my bedside stool.

Just for tonight, that's all . . .

I breathe out and carefully push back the bedsheet. Pull Tyndale's Bible towards me. My fingers tremor on the spine. Dread churns through me. This is insane. This is heresy. A

44

death sentence. What on earth am I doing?

Just a small peek . . .

I clench my jaw and open the first page. On Tyndale's title page, where the printer's name and address should normally lie, are the proud words PRINTED IN UTOPIA.

The laughter stutters out of me. Imagine Thomas More being brought a printed copy. Licking his greedy lips and drooling over the heresies hidden within. Eagerly unwrapping the paper parcel. Opening it. Reading the first page.

Just imagine his face!

My fingertips tremble on the paper. I shut my eyes, take a deep breath and turn to a random page. Somewhere near the middle. I open my eyes again, looking everywhere except down at the words. But that niggling urge, that gnawing impulse . . . finally, I drag my gaze onto the page.

In the begynnynge
was that worde

I drop it as if scalded. The Bible falls to the floor with a soft leathery thump as I shrink against the headboard, breathing hard. Bess turns over, mumbles, then sinks back into blissful

45

sleep. My head throbs: a woman died for this today! A man chanted these words before the towering pyre, his last gasps of defiance before they beat him down and dragged him away.

I swallow and crawl to the edge of the bed. Hesitate. Then reach out and scoop it up. Turn to that fateful page once more . . .

and that worde was with god: and god was thatt worde. The same was in the begynnynge wyth god.

My heart clenches; I know these words! I can finally read this! Every single line!

And so can my children.

The realisation leaves me awestruck, a sudden surge of breathless joy. I imagine Joan perched on Bess's lap, her small hand tracing the beautiful gold-leafed illuminations as Bess reads aloud to her.

For decades past, our forefathers have endured dreary Latin sermons droned from distant church pulpits, the dull foreign words washing over their heads, every one a mystery far beyond their reach. Not for us to ever understand, only to sit and passively listen, deaf to God's true word.

Not anymore.

Dawn finds me hammering on Poyntz's door. Cranton lets me inside, stifling a yawn. 'Blimey, Mark. It's barely seven!'

In the hidden meeting room the men are gazing over a large map. Tyndale looks up and smiles. 'Mark! To what do we owe the pleasure?'

I place the book before him. 'I've read enough. I want to help. I want in.'

Silence; then the others gather around me, thumping my back heartily and murmuring their approval. Tyndale beams at me, then claps his hands. 'Gentlemen! You all know your roles tonight. Robert and Harry will be our seamen for this evening.' Two weatherbeaten men salute him from across the table, grinning yellow smiles and reeking of salt as Tyndale continues: 'No Channel ports tonight. Keep it quiet. I trust in your absolute discretion.'

He raises a hand and gazes around at us all, eyes glistening with proud tears. 'Tonight's the night, friends. For far too long we've been running and hiding.' He hugs the Bible to his heart. 'Now let's bring this book home!'

Vaughan steps forward. Cracks his knuckles. 'We're with you, William!' The others roar their approval and pour out the room with newfound purpose, chatting and laughing.

At the doorway Vaughan pulls me aside. 'You look changed, Mark. What convinced you?'

I smile. 'John's Gospel. Chapter One.'

Vaughan pats my shoulder. 'Good man.' He motions towards the window, at the bustle of street life outside. 'Most people blunder around this city and all they see are streets. Shops. Other people. When you walk with Tyndale long enough, you see the battlefield.' He pauses, gives me a long searching look. 'You've seen it already, haven't you?

I bristle. 'How do you know that?'

'You were an army surgeon, right? Tom told me all about it. Italy, weren't you?'

I clench my jaw. 'Yes.'

'Any good?'

'Good enough.'

Vaughan nods sagely. 'Seen a lot of awful injuries, then,' he murmurs. 'Violent deaths.'

I blink away the images. 'Plenty.'

His eyes crease in sympathy. 'Bit of trouble too, I bet. Lots of danger?'

I sigh heavily. 'Of course, yes. Seen more than enough for one lifetime. Far too much.'

A long sombre pause. Then Vaughan's eyes twinkle, a dangerous gleam of excitement. 'Want to see some more?

I breathe out. 'Oh *God*, yes.'

A cool cloudless summer night. The boat keel scrapes ashore. We splash through foaming surf up the moonlit beach, pebbles crunching beneath our sodden boots as Robert and Harry lead the way.

A deserted beach. One of the little inlets of East Anglia; those hidden tidal creeks where a small boat with dubious cargo can be beached by moonlight, unloaded and swiftly pushed out to sea again, with no one the wiser.

'John boy,' Harry calls softly. Nothing at first, then two hooded shadows melt out of the whispering dune grass ahead. As they approach they lower their hoods: burly bearded men carrying shuttered lanterns.

'Evenin', gents,' the taller man grins with a flash of crooked teeth. 'Nice night for it, eh?' They lead us behind the dunes to a sunken dirt road. A horse-drawn wagon awaits us before the marshland. We heave the bales of cloth on board, the printed sheets of Tyndale's New Testament safe between thick folded linen. Nestled warm and dry, God whispers within each wrapped bundle. The drivers climb up, wave farewell and move off, the dray wagon bumping over the rough earthen track.

We trail back towards the beach with much grinning and back-slapping. At the crest of the dune I halt, gazing over the peaceful scene. The soft hiss of the waves, the distant mournful wail of a curlew hidden in the marsh, reeds rustling in the night breeze. A jarringly loud bark of laughter as the others haul the boats back into the shallows, already knee-deep in black choppy waves. Whitecaps gleam silver in the moonlight.

'All right, Mark?' Harry calls from the nearest stern. 'You coming?'

I wave back. 'Just a minute!' I gaze over the scene: the rowers waiting in the churning surf, ready to cast off back into the lion's jaws; the dray cart trundling off, headed for Bishopsgate by dawn towards London's beating heart. Suddenly a warm surge of gladness washes over me like gentle summer rain. All of these people are everyday common folk living out their ordinary, mundane and commonplace lives – merchant sailors, wagoners, innkeepers – yet all prepared to put their lives in mortal danger over a simple book. For the sake of their children. Their grandchildren.

My heart swells with pride. There's a cause worth fighting for. But worth dying for?

Absolutely.

Under the Emperor's brutal laws, my brothers and sisters are slaughtered for their faith, the men beheaded and the women buried alive. If caught printing without a license, perhaps it's your eye gouged out, a hand hacked off, the hiss of the burning brand and the foul stench of roasting flesh, your belly slashed open and your guts fed to dogs.

But they can't lock us all up. They have prisons enough for bodies, yes. But an idea? It's impossible to eradicate. They can seize our goods, but God will provide. They may close down the booksellers and burn the woodcuts, but still there will be books. When the Emperor's troopers come searching, battering down our doors with axes and sledgehammers – and they will – we'll confound them all. False drawers. Dusty compartments underneath floorboards. Bread ovens. Straw mangers. Hidden cupboards behind wainscots. Attics. Haylofts. Cellars. If they uncover one hiding place, we'll simply make another. They can keep their mouldering old bones, their marble saints and gold shrines, their priests and prayers.

But we have the printing press.

God's voice will cross the Narrow Sea again, unloaded through the Channel ports and seeping into England's heartland. Black-market Bibles selling for two shillings each, selling like smuggled rum in shady corners and on hidden back-alley doorsteps. Already six thousand were safely in England last week, long before the scholars and bishops even knew what was happening. They'll never stop this floodtide of faith, never suppress Tyndale's words. No chance. With every passing month the old certainties are chipped away – nowhere in the scriptures does it mention penances or purgatory, relics or rituals or rosary beads. Show us where it says monks or nuns. Wherever does it say 'Pope'?

So what, if England's bishops scorn us and besmirch us? Let Bishop Tunstall breathe hellfire on us from his lofty Durham pulpit. Let Bishop Stokesley, London's scourge of heretics, label us filthy swine and Satan's shit. Let Thomas More and Stephen Gardiner sneer that Tyndale's Bible is an ignorant smear of blasphemy riddled with errors. Let them hold their monopoly of Latin, the exclusive privilege of nobles, popes, clerics and kings. Excuses. Just feeble excuses to hoard God all to themselves, not share Him about with the common folk. 'Too precious,' they bleat. 'Pearls trampled under the hooves of swine,' they protest. What do we care? Here's the Word of God in our own hands at last, in our very own English language. Everyone deserves to hear God's voice for themselves, even the lowliest ploughboy and shepherd grubbing the earth – you won't need years in the priesthood for that. No wonder they're angry. Scared. Vengeful.

But Charles will never win. He offers his subjects nothing but more pain, misery and suffering. He and the Holy Church claim to think for many people, but they don't ever think *of* them. And if there is indeed a God, He would never rejoice at the burnings, beheadings, maimings and beatings committed in His name by intolerant fanatics. He would celebrate the very best we could be, not condone the worst we are. Men, not beasts. Angels, not monsters. The Emperor offers people only agony, terror and unending despair.

But Tyndale? He offers them hope.

We few are small and hidden, scattered and weakened in our isolated enclaves. But together we are united, and strong. Far stronger than these liars in the dark, huddled in the dusty comfort of their cold towering churches with their wine and roast venison, shrouded in dogma and tradition, wrapped in their gold-fringed silks, velvet robes and satin vestments. Charles wants to keep Europe trapped under his thumb forever with superstition, fear and torment? He has plans for people? Well, Tyndale has dreams for them.

We may not live to see Sunday. Even tomorrow, they might storm in, arrest us all, drag us away to rot in prison. I may not see the sunset. But no going out on their terms, paraded through the jeering streets to an agonising end at the stake. I'll go out swinging, blade in hand, on my own terms.

Besides, Tyndale's book will still see the new dawn.

You can burn men, and you can burn books. But the truth won't burn, no more than water or milk. We'll have ten thousand copies safely in England before this week's out. They might as well try and gather up the stars as to keep all those out of the hands of God's own people. Can't be done. The truth can't be unheard. Can't be unseen. Can't be unsaid. The more dissidents they clap behind bars and the more books they burn, the more people will be crowded at their gates shouting 'What's so important about this? Whatever are you hiding from us? What are we missing?' They will never stopper up God's mouth for good – not now He's able to speak to us face to face Himself, in Tyndale's plain English.

And God said, Let there be light: and there was light.

Want to see what freedom looks like? Watch us.

SPYMASTER

The prisoner huddles in the dark, far from the flickering torchlight as he can, as if hoping to melt away into a crack and slither through the mortar gaps to freedom.

Fat chance here, Francis thinks, easing back in his chair. Walls three feet thick. Solid stone blocks, neither crack nor crevasse. Four floors up, too. What's his miraculous plan then? Sprout wings and fly over the Tower walls? Unlikely. Not with crossbowmen roaming the battlements.

His ruff itches; he scratches his neck absently, gazing down at the shrivelled tangle of limbs in a grimy undershirt, the pathetic prisoner who cringes away from the torchlight like a whipped mongrel. His men wait by the door; Arthur Gregory sits ready with inkwell and paper, Thomas Rogers leans against the wall in black tunic and hose, totally at ease. By contrast Antony Babington's hair is filthy and matted, his unshaven face creased in sorrow; he looks like a scrap of half-chewed gristle left on the side of a trencher. The long nights here have aged him a decade, though he's still only twenty-four.

'Antony.' His voice cleaves the silence; Babington shudders. 'Antony, be sensible. We know your crimes. Your guilt. You know the penalty for plotting to contrive the queen's death, to place her cousin on the throne.'

'Who says?' Babington twists to face him, glaring beneath his ragged curtain of hair. 'Heresy? Who dares name me traitor?'

'Her majesty the queen, all of Christian England, Almighty God . . . and me.' His voice flows on like warm honey, low, soothing, certain. He watches Babington's face change, sliding into confusion, gnawing doubt, and finally – as the stark truths are slowly unveiled before him – to ashen-faced terror. The messages smuggled into Chartley Hall inside a beer barrel. The barrel intercepted, the hollow bung broken open. He arranged the whole deception, and let these fools seize the bait; hook, line and sinker. Let Antony fear that he is all-seeing, all-knowing. Can't hurt, surely. He keeps talking, lets the words wash over the prisoner and crumble his resolve like wet sand. He can do this all day, talk on and on with simple, unyielding truths until his captives plead for mercy. No mercy here, though. Not in the Tower. Not for high treason.

'You . . . you read Mary's letters?' Babington eventually croaks. 'All of them? How?'

He rolls his eyes. 'Don't you know? I read everyone's letters.' Including yours.

'But . . . but they were never tampered with. The seals weren't ever broken.'

Ah, that's where you're wrong. Arthur and Thomas figured it out last spring. All they needed was a heated knife, a blob of wax, a decent sigil forgery to reseal it, a delicate touch and extraordinary patience. Which you idiots never had.

Walls have ears, and shadows have eyes. He, William Cecil and Robert Dudley are the hidden thorns, sharp as daggers, guarding England's pure virgin rose Eliza. The queen and her noblemen sleep in new houses of rosy brick, or feast in old manors whose fortifications have crumbled away. England has enjoyed twenty-five sunny years of hard-won peace, won not by the boom of cannons or the clash of swords, but the scratch of the pen, the crackle of unfurled parchment, the clatter of rider's hooves. His duties are so manifold, the scope of his job so ill-defined, ever changing like shifting marshland beneath your feet. This suits him just fine. Lord Chancellor Thomas Bromley is anchored fast by his heavy chain of office, and the eyes of Master Treasurer Knollys cannot stray far from the queen's private chests of fat gold sovereigns, but plain Mr Secretary can inquire into any grand office of state he chooses, worm his way into any hidden corner of government with Eliza's blessing. All the affairs of the realm are whispered in his ear; his offices are so plural and far-reaching under the Crown that all the great business of England flows across his desk, parchment and scroll awaiting stamp or signet. The statutes of England – every precedent and clause – are safely stowed in his head, neatly filed alongside the columns of the queen's account ledgers and the lineage, acreage and income of every English gentleman.

But information is worth more than gold or gems, and in the murky underworld of state espionage, he is its true king. The memory swims into view: his elder brother Edmund clapping him on the back with a chortle of, 'Never make the excuse, "You can't see behind closed doors." Find out, little brother.'

So he has. A vast web of intelligence stretches from the storm-lashed cliffs of Galway to the sweltering alleyways of Constantinople, the air heavy with saffron and cloves, nutmeg and cinnamon; from the chilly streets of Hamburg to the rolling hills of sun-kissed Tuscany, to the arid shore of Algiers with its flat honey-brown rooftops. Informants, ciphers and double agents, whispers, scribblings and plots all across Europe – did you really believe a second-rate manor house in Derbyshire would escape our notice, Antony? With its rose gardens, its dovecote, its hidden cellar vaults?

'In August last year, John Ballard and Thomas Morgan were your guests at Dethick Manor. Two weeks later they dined with you again. I wonder what was discussed?'

'Bollocks to that,' Babington sneers – the young cub still has claws yet, a hidden spark of rebellious spirit. 'You'll get no admission from me.'

He shrugs. 'I don't need one. The serving girl who carried in the honeyed plums, she was mine. The scullion boy who carved the beef, he was mine too. They talked about the French League, the foreign armies awaiting your signal, how King Philip himself had blessed this enterprise.' He watches Babington's sneer fade, his eyes widen in disbelief. He doesn't say, we hear things because we listen, we see them because we watch.

A hidden army of unseen eavesdroppers waits vigilant under his command; potboys and kennelmen, washerwomen and chambermaids, grooms and cupbearers beneath notice or suspicion. He knows when to charm and bribe, to coax and comfort, to threaten or flatter. His wards, servants and young men can slip unseen into any room like a wisp of smoke; these unscholarly, unlettered boys have sharper ears and eyes than even the landowning gentry. Money and gentle words buy silence more than threats or the fist. He doesn't say, your man Gifford has been on my payroll for the past eight months now, and you had no idea. Gilbert

Gifford is a shrewd, devious man. You don't know how he will turn to safeguard his own fortunes. He has been paid fifty pounds this year to shelter beneath the Walsingham wing.

Babington is shaking with rage and fear. 'Your usurper's light is fading. Mary's the monarch England needs – she'll deliver this land back to true religion!'

Arthur's pen scratches. Francis closes his eyes: what religion is that? One of blood, fire and sword, corpses twisting in the breeze at Tyburn, the stench of burnt meat and a pall of human ash hanging over Smithfield. Only thirty years since Ridley, Latimer and Cranmer were fed to the flames. If you're lucky the breeze is low, the sheaves of straw stacked high about your waist, the kindling beneath you bone dry. It's over in a few heartbeats of searing agony. Wrapped in a sheet of flame, consumed by blistering heat, your soul ascends to the clouds in a sigh of smoke.

If you're lucky.

They weren't. It was an awful botched mess drawn out for public spectacle, that churning grey October morning in Oxford. The fresh green faggots smouldering and crackling; the vagrant fickle wind blowing the flames away from the condemned; smoke billowing over the weeping angels of Balliol College and coiling through the maws of dragons on Trinity's North Tower; the stray dogs of Magdelen Street and Cornmarket whimpering at the stench of burning flesh. Almost three hundred poor Protestant souls fed Bloody Mary's fanaticism barely a generation ago.

When will this meaningless slaughter ever end? Protestants and Catholics have been at each other's throats for decades now. Elizabeth's half-sister became a monster once she seized the throne. Then St Bartholomew's Day – it's been over ten years, yet their screams still haunt his dreams at night. The Huguenots pleading for mercy as the bloody axes hacked down, the roars of drunken rioters, the streets of Paris awash with gore. Women, children, babes, the elderly. No one spared, all for the crime of believing the Pope can sometimes be wrong, and that you don't need gilded trappings to worship God; not gold leaf or jewelled crosses, chantries or marble statues or gilded paintings, the whiff of incense or droning Latin sermons. Nowhere in the scriptures does it mention purgatory and penances and popes, reliquaries and rosary beads. But just try reminding papists that – see how far it gets you before they come baying for your blood.

What is England, now? An isle of ghosts whispering in the night, amid the damp fenland marshes of the east and the stony crags of the west. The dead do not rise again. That is a privilege reserved for one man only, and if good King Arthur has not seen fit to disturb his slumbers through these scorched centuries of catastrophe, it is not for us to wake him. Yet if the dead do not rise, they do return to haunt our dreams: bones singing beneath the high altars, leaching through clay into water, lapping at our foundations. The rustle of bridal sheet or funeral shroud, a buried empire of ghosts clustered around holy wells rustling like fallen leaves; all those unseen dead warming their bones around forges and fireside hearths in winter. Always a feather's breath from the living, like a fragrant wreath of incense, like a sigh misting glass.

There is far too much history crammed into this dark sour soil for a body to rest easy within it. In sweltering July heat he has kneeled before the carved tombs of ancestors, stone Garter Knights armoured head to toe in steel plate and chainmail, gauntleted hands clasped in prayer, stub-fingered and snub-nosed by the endless kiss of time. Good King Henry of Monmouth, fifth of that name, frozen in carved black oak in the golden prime of his manhood, just shy of thirty-six. Barely a hundred feet away, Henry Tudor lies in gilt bronze alongside his beloved wife, liberator of England from the tyranny of King Crookback. Elizabeth is a true-born Tudor; she has inherited her grandfather's iron stomach for war, her father's love of lavish grandeur and spectacle. The courtly pageants, the Virgin Queen's countryside progress from manor house to stately castle with her royal entourage.

Under her reign there is a new England reborn; from the honeyed praise of her diplomats and foreign ambassadors you would think it a tranquil realm of miracles, a happy land of plenty where the cobblestones to London are nuggets of gold and even the smallest brooks flow rich with claret.

He knows better. Dispatches pour in every day with yet more grim news from the shires. A miserable wet summer has led to repeated harvest failures, wheat and barley rotting away in sodden fields. Profiteers are already hoarding grain and charging exorbitant fees. The price of wheat is forecast to rise to thirty-five shillings a quarter – more than double that of two years ago – and the townsfolk's bellies growl ever louder. In Shoreditch only last year, four Londoners were crushed to death fighting over a dole of bread. A shame that the queen's loyal subjects should starve. Pestilence still clings on with its grimy claws; a fresh outbreak of plague is bubbling through Chesterfield in Derbyshire. Over March Lent this year, gaol fever ripped through the prison at Exeter. Eight justices of the peace and the Sheriff of Devon dead. War with Spain and rebellions in Ireland are draining England's coffers fast. The months have run away from him like a flurry of autumn leaves skittering towards winter; the glorious summer is past, and hard days lie ahead. Riots, discontent, and famine before the spring. But no use waiting for the Lord Chancellor to feed his people. Bromley can't boil an egg.

This is England, then: a huddled mass of ghosts peering over your shoulder like gawpers at a market fair, the Faithful Departed watching your every move, sniggering at your every mistake. Picture Albion: a sorry offshore island, damp and cold, guarded by the glorious dead, led by a bewigged and bejewelled figurehead already past fifty. And he its sworn defender, plunging his hands daily into the filth so that the realm stays clean. Someone must.

He consults his papers. 'Antony, you have been in treasonous company where the queen has been called a painted whore.'

Antony scoffs. 'Is this the best slander you can conjure up?'

'You have said, the queen would see this country burn if she could rule over the ashes, she disdains the realm to gain yet more power.'

Antony rolls his eyes.

'Have you not said, "All the queen's pomp and majesty cannot hide her poxy face?" It is true that Gloriana is slowly losing her looks, the faded scars of smallpox shrouded beneath her white-plastered mask. But the cracks are already beginning to show, in his realm, his England, his queen.

Not that he'll ever admit that to Antony.

'Have you not said, "Once Elizabeth dies, then farewell Master Walsingham"? Have you not said, "Why wait for Elizabeth to spawn an heir when we have a ready prince in Scotland, the whole Tudor line is doomed"?'

Antony flushes. 'I don't deal in curses,' he sneers.

'No,' he smiles. 'Women's gossip.' He waits, lets the tense hush lengthen, stretch almost to snapping point, then: 'Perhaps your wife does?'

Silence.

'How is Margery, by the way?'

Silence. *Now* Antony looks afraid.

He studies his fingernails. 'How should I explain your predicament? If you refuse to give evidence and a court finds you guilty of such heinous treason, then the queen will curse your family name, strip away all your wealth and inheritance and hand them to someone with proven loyalty.'

Babington juts out his chin. 'She wouldn't dare. The queen respects all ancient lands and titles.'

'Then let's say *I* will.' He rises from his seat; backlit, his monstrous shadow swallows the cell floor. Babington whimpers and scrabbles against the wall, a mongrel shrinking from the sting of the lash. 'Let's say I will rip your life apart, right here and now, tonight. Me and my boys.' Antony Babington, second-rate lawyer, gentleman's heir, heretic and simpering court toady, meet Francis Walsingham: Principal Secretary to her majesty the queen, Lord Privy Seal, knight of the realm and Spymaster General; England's wolf against papism, defender of the true faith, master of whisperers, ruffians and cutthroats, and MP for Surrey. When his busy schedule permits.

Babington bares his teeth from the flagstones. 'So what now? You'll torture me, will you? They say you broke John Ballard yourself.'

'Ballard? That pathetic priest?' He shrugs. 'I never laid a finger on him.' I can't answer for my lads, though. The whisper down Eastcheap is that they placed him on the rack and pulled, pulled, pulled, until he sang like a bird. His bloody lips cracked open and your name oozed out. And others. John Travers. Jerome Bellamy. John Charnock. Robert Gage. Noblemen's heirs. Courtiers. Traitors all.

He motions towards Thomas lounging against the wall. 'You see this lad? You think him a pleasant sort? Would you like to spend ten minutes alone with him?'

Thomas grins and saunters forward into the light, cracking his knuckles. 'Five would do.'

Babington glowers at Thomas, who waves

back. 'So that's why he's here, is it?' His face twists in disgust. 'Another lowborn churl of yours, so you'll never sully your own hands?'

His hand curls into a fist. 'Shall I refresh your memory? Tom here was once a humble page in your lord father's service. He said the Eucharist host was but a piece of bread, and your father Sir Henry had him stripped and beaten before the household – ah, I see that frown, I see this tale is familiar to you – with the menservants jeering and the young girls sniggering behind their hands.'

Thomas Rogers was barely a child then, when he came stumbling through the gates of his house on Seething Lane and collapsed sobbing against Walsingham's shoulder. He still whimpers in his sleep even now, at twenty-eight. Not from the pain; every child can bear their master's wrath. From his nakedness. His humiliation in the shivering cold, while the gentle ladies tittered, the infant girls giggled and the rod slashed red welts over his quaking buttocks. 'And now? Tom Rogers is in my service, under my protection, and the bravest lad I know.'

He sees the boy's thin face blush with pleasure, and feels a fond wave of pride: I took him in when he was a pitiful orphan flinching at shadows, and look at how he's blossomed – Thomas Rogers, once scorned and downtrodden among the Babington swine, now a fiercely loyal servant, expert forger and bloodhound of traitors; his manners faultless, kind and cheerful to chambermaids and potboys, polite and respectful to his elders, graciously charming to virgin girls, gentle to infants. He understands honour and duty yet never boasts of his own, and if a demon ever crept inside to frighten Walsingham's grandnieces in their Barn Elms beds, Tom would kick it downstairs horns-over-hooves onto its hairy arse. He has no illusions about the world, but he still has hopes. His French is flawless, his Spanish is excellent, and his German . . . well, his German is right where it was. Nobody's perfect.

He crouches down before his defiant captive. 'Antony, relieve yourself of this burden. If your confession is full, honest, clear and unsparing, the queen may be inclined to show mercy.'

Babington's lip curls. 'And if I refuse? You won't torture gentlemen. The queen would never allow it.'

He smiles, skewers Babington with a glare.

'What Elizabeth doesn't know won't hurt her.' Viper-quick, his hands snap forward and clamp Babington's skull tight, thumbs poised over the prisoner's eyes. His voice hardens, a blade hacking ice. 'I only need to press down, and you'll sing whatever song I choose to hear. Understand?'

He releases his grip, lets Babington slump into the straw, white-faced with terror. 'You're a Christian man, and yet you say this?' Antony bleats. 'You dare deceive me with lies of mercy?'

He shrugs. 'I don't know the queen's mind. I can only speak for my own. She may grant you clemency as a young courtier, a nobleman's heir led astray by sordid whispers. Or not. Perhaps she'll let you live abroad, disgraced, exiled and penniless, but alive. She may grant you mercy as to the manner of your death. Or not. The traitor's penalty is fearful and public, he dies in great pain and public humiliation – ah, I see you *do* know, you've witnessed it before.'

It's a slow agonising ordeal; strangled by the choking noose, your feet dancing and jerking in the breeze; cut down still alive and castrated, then leisurely gutted by the executioner. No hurry. People like a show. Your manhood sizzling in a brazier, the stench of burnt meat clogging your nose as the knife rips through your bowels, before your entrails are pulled out and waved over a roaring crowd. Then the final swift shock of the axe, the sweeping carpet of blood. And then it's all over. People bring their infant children to gawp, swaying on their shoulders. Some pray. Some jeer. Some munch yeast buns. Will there be pies on sale?

Nothing protects you. On the scaffold at Tyburn, beneath the hangman's blades, neither rank nor kin, wealth nor deeds. An open field where streets seep into pasture, now trampled to mud, awash with snarling faces. Nothing between you and the ravenous mob roaring for its pound of flesh. Babington shrinks away, arms folded across his chest as if shielding his guts from the butcher's knife, and he thinks: poor foolish Babington, you never had a chance. He'd once glimpsed Mary swirling through Chartley gardens with her ladies-in-waiting; her fiery red mane, her icy-blue eyes flashing, her serpent gaze. She is utterly without remorse; there's no crime she would not commit to further her ruthless ambitions, pampered, arrogant and stubbornly assured of her birthright. And you, poor pining boy, were too proud, too reckless to bend with the breeze, too gullible to think a young pretender to the English throne would even spare a glance towards you.

He sighs, turns to his ward. 'Will you fetch the frame, Tom?'

'The frame?' Thomas frowns. 'What's that?'

'That vice to clamp the limb before we break it. Just downstairs, on the right.' Antony shudders behind him.

Thomas glances down at the prisoner. 'I'm sure, sir,' he tells Babington, 'that you wouldn't wish my lord to go to all that trouble . . .'

Antony scuttles back against the wall. 'Mother Mary protect me!' he whimpers.

'She won't.' Francis stifles a yawn. Outside the moon is rising, white bars creeping across the flagstones. His mind keeps straying back home to Seething Lane, torchlight spilling out of the house; Ursula awaiting on his doorstep with folded arms and a scowl of 'Working late again?' He'll miss her supper again, for sure. Maybe he can buy her something nice before Michaelmas. Those blue velvet sleeves from Italy, as an apology? Worth a try. He knows the right people in Florence and Venice. He'll get it done.

'Enough of this,' he tells Thomas, 'I'm tired. Fetch the mallets as well, Tom.'

He settles back to Mary's letters, Phelippes' cipher laid out beside them. The problem with Mary, he's decided, is that she's far too proud for her own damn good. Her brazen arrogance on proclaiming her true birthright to England's throne, her sniggers with her handmaidens over Elizabeth's barren womb. And all the while Thomas Phelippes was eavesdropping close by, stooped among the flowerbeds with a rake in hand, straw hat hiding his face.

Antony is trying to shrink himself smaller on his pad of straw. His shoulders are hunched, his eyes closed. Lay a hand on his shoulder and you would feel every nerve jumping in terror.

Thomas appears in the doorway. 'Is this what you wanted, sir? The frame's on its way up.'

He had imagined a short wooden-headed mallet, for tapping in the wedges to hold the limb rigid. What Thomas has brought in is another instrument entirely, with a stout ash handle three feet long and a blunt steel head larger than a clenched fist. A weapon, not a tool. He stands up and takes it from Thomas, smiling. 'Where did you find it? You could smash down a warhorse with this thing.' The hammer's head is cold against his palm. The blunt unforgiving edges. Crushing. Pulverising.

Antony moans. They both look down at him. Thomas chews his lip. 'Too much?'

'What? No no, of course not.' He pats Thomas's shoulder. 'This'll do just fine.' He holds out the hammer at arm's length, above the flagstones. Then he drops his arm and swings it, testing the heavy weight, enjoying the whoosh of air. He likes the sensation. The pleasant sway of the body; the moment of balance, control, then the growing impulse, the gnawing childlike eagerness that whispers: 'Swing it! Swing it!' A warm giddiness, such as you might feel with your first woman: a delicate lightness at the point of no return.

The clang when the hammer hits the wall is loud enough to wake the dead. It sweeps Antony's feet from under him, jerks him back into the corner. 'Jesus!'

'He won't help you.' He props the hammer against the wall, crouches before his prisoner. 'No one wants your screams, Antony. They're of no use to us. I don't want your pain, I want words that make sense. Or else . . .' he nods at

Arthur poised with pen and ink. 'Words can be built on your silence. They will be.' He shakes his head sadly. Straightens up. 'You love your children, don't you?'

Antony's head jerks up, like a startled deer. Naked terror in his eyes. 'What did you do?'

'Oh, nothing.' Yet. 'Edward and Mary, isn't it?' Two squalling babes squirming in their cradles, wailing for their missing father. 'Do you think it's clever to leave a wife without company, a son without guidance, a daughter without protection?'

Antony hangs his head as he continues: 'I can't save you, Antony. You have chosen your dreadful end, and must endure. I cannot change your fate.'

His voice softens. 'But you can save *theirs*.'

Antony raises his head. A glimmer of desperate yearning in teary eyes. Imagine what small mercies you could give a condemned man, to make him weep and break his will, let his words flow free – instead of what you could rip away. Offer him something to live for, or a death that spares him shame, saves him agony. Every man wants something, if only for the endless pain to stop.

'The queen is not a heartless monster, Antony. She is not without compassion or mercy. She will settle your debts and provide for your family. Give us names, and their safety is assured. Margery will grow old cared for and nurtured by your children. They need not be reviled, penniless, cast out on the road to grovel in destitution.'

He lets the silence lengthen, then: 'But if you don't name the others, then you will die alone and unmourned, and they're going to move on without you. All of them. Mary will grow up, and she's going to walk down the aisle to another man. And you won't be there. Your wife is going to find someone else, and your son will go wooing for his bride. But you won't see any of it. The weddings. The christenings. The birthdays. Your grandchildren in their cradles. You're going to miss *everything*.'

Antony stares up at him, beseeching. 'You promise not to touch my family?' he whispers.

'I would *never* harm your family. I swear it.' He squeezes Antony's shoulder. 'But how will they remember you, in the years to come? As an ignoble traitor who had forsaken his vows with stubborn silence, or a brave father who let his family thrive beyond his death, rather than drag them all down with him? Which is it, Antony – a broken coward, or a good man?'

Antony scrabbles against the wall. 'Please . . . I swear to God –'

'Swear to *me*.'

With a groan of defeat Antony turns to the wall, names tumbling from his lips as Arthur's pen captures them all – Travers, Charnock, Bellamy, Gage. And others; John Savage, Robert Barnewell, Charles Tilney, Edward Abington, Henry Dunn. Thomas Salisbury. Ballard babbled their names in a dungeon cell dripping with chill, and now Babington has damned his compatriots himself with sweet green words of confession, as the dread wormed inside his belly and sank its claws deep.

Outside, Tom leans against the wall, eyes brimming with tears. 'You said, fetch the frame.' He sniffles wetly. 'I thought, Mother Mary, whatever does he mean, I don't know of any frame, what should I *do*?'

'Hey.' He cups Tom's cheek, as tender as any father soothing his son's hurts. 'You're doing beautifully. I'm so proud of you.' He reaches out and curls both arms around Tom's shoulders.

Tom inhales sharply, and then something deep inside just . . . *crumbles*. His arms are wrapped tight around Francis, his hands fisted in Francis's tunic. His shoulders quake, his breath stutters and hitches as Francis holds him close, rubbing his back as Tom buries his face into his shoulder. He can do this, can hold Tom close and rub slow gentle circles across his back until his shoulders stop shaking.

The corridor is cold and quiet, as Tom weeps in his arms. Eventually, Tom's heaving shudders cease and the tension in his shoulders slowly ebbs away. He pulls back, scrubbing a hand across his eyes. 'Sorry.'

'Don't be.' Francis squeezes his shoulder. 'Not everyone has the stomach for this. You were brilliant tonight. Go get some rest.'

Tom chuckles wetly as Arthur ruffles his hair. They watch him wobble down the corridor, still a little shaky. Muffled sobbing echoes from the cell behind them. There is no damage to the prisoner, not even a scrape to his shins. Arthur still glances back, uneasy. 'Would you have used it? The rack? The hammer?'

A guttering torch flickers in its wall bracket. Water drips somewhere, eating into the dull stone. The faint clank of manacles. The smell's always the worst here: enclosed stale air, the metallic tang of blood, the sour reek of piss seeping into the floor. 'I mean to say,' Arthur sighs, 'could . . . could you smash a man's limbs to paste, and then go home to supper with your family?'

He shakes his head. 'I haven't got a family back home. Just the wife.' His only living daughter, Frances, is over in Flanders now.

'No,' Arthur corrects himself, blushing. 'Begging your pardon, sir.'

'Although,' he smiles remembering Liz, that naked squalling armful of flailing fists, 'I am a grandfather now.'

'But still, with Ballard . . .' Arthur scuffs the floor. He wasn't there that fateful day, when Ballard was hauled in. 'It's a mighty sin, to rack a chained man.'

'Which is why it never happened. I never ordered it. And never will.'

'But . . . but the rumours . . .'

'Alehouse gossip, that's all. People like gory tales, so I obliged them.' He smiles at the amazement that washes across Arthur's face; let the rumours seep out into Cheapside taverns and the brothels of Southwark; let them be enlarged, misheard, embellished, misunderstood. No one was hurt in his pursuit of the truth – he sat in a room and simply talked, that's all. Planted terrors in a traitor's head then let his own gnawing fear destroy him; dangled a thread of hope before his eyes and let him snatch at it with starving claws. Worked on Ballard, worked on Babington. He is willing to pinch a man with pain, but he sees it as a failing if he has to call for heated irons and pliers; the mere threat itself will accomplish far more. None of us can withstand anything, really. Scrape the skin and beneath it there is always a raw naked infant, howling.

But then he threw Antony a precious lifeline, a sliver of salvation for his family; if you want to utterly crush a man, show him despair. But if you want him to yield you everything, to pour out his soul and spill every vile secret clasped to his bosom, offer him hope.

It still amazes him, sometimes, what plain words can do.

Arthur stares at his boots. 'I've seen people strung up. By their wrists.'

'Sooner or later you see everything.' There's a heavy aching weight deep in his chest, like the hammer head. He'd like to swing the hammer again, that precious flicker of boyish glee. The steel head was large so it barely jarred the wall. 'You have his confession?'

Arthur flourishes the bundle of papers with a triumphant smirk. 'Every word.' Then his grin fades. 'But . . . will the queen do it? Have him executed? He still comes from a noble house.'

'No matter. The queen's done a number of things that have never been done before.'

Arthur nods. 'Hasn't done the dungeon work, though.'

True. Or mopped the floor of blood and vomit afterwards. Or shaken clinging flesh from chains, out on the execution scaffold at Holborn. Nasty grim work, keeping the peace for the Lioness of England. Takes a strong stomach to do it. Just as Henry Tudor came for the salvation of Albion, with a broom to sweep out the charred bones and a rag to mop up the gore.

I know how you feel, Henry, he thinks. Weary to the bone. He frowns at Arthur. 'What tempted you into this sordid business?'

Arthur shrugs, tucks the sheaf of papers under one arm. 'Man's got to earn a living.'

'You could have been an honest farmer

instead.'

Arthur rolls his eyes. 'And do what? Kill pigs?'

Sow seed, that's what he meant. Reap the grain at harvest. Maybe plant an apple orchard. Harmless pursuits, breathing new life into the earth. There is a pure clean paradise somewhere where men live on milk and honey, the bread so white and soft it's like eating sunlight. Far beyond this damp isle of mud, blood and shit. He'll never reach that blessed heaven with all the sins weighing upon his damned soul. Arthur won't, either. But perhaps their grandchildren will. Maybe. Some day.

He feels restless, already impatient for the soft warmth of home. Riding through the gates as his household swarm around him with their flushed smiling faces. His kennelmaster wrapping him in a bone-crushing hug with a jubilant roar of 'Here's the man in charge!' His cook's giggling daughters dashing along the upper landings with the greyhounds clattering alongside, their paws scrabbling on the floorboards. A blackbird singing from the rose garden, the air scented with rosemary and camomile. His servants cheerfully heckling each other over their chopping boards as the aroma of baked apples wafts out into the hallway. A city house that breathes comfort, always smelling of cakes. His wife smiling fondly as she snuffs out the bedside candle, draws back the sheet. 'Come to bed, love.'

He has all this awaiting him. What does Antony have?

He gazes down at the weeping wretch and thinks: your life won't end with a glorious martyr's death, Antony, revered down the ages in hushed whispers. It will end amid the foul stench of shit and burnt meat, the sour reek of piss, flinching from the peltings of rotten food, the jeering crowd pushing and shoving for a better view as the hangman chops off your manhood, slits your belly open and yanks out your innards as the mob roars for blood. Your name will sink into infamy; you shall be forever derided and mocked, tossed out on the dunghill of history. Rewarded as a traitor deserves. There is a time to hold steadfast to your beliefs, to harbour secret delusions of wooing and yearning, to smirk behind your hidden hand of cards, but there is also a time to throw your purse down on the table and concede: 'Enough, Master Walsingham. Game over. You win.'

FIREBRAND

He kneels in the damp straw, checks the fuse for a third time. *Stop fussing, you idiot*, he scolds himself, *you're just nervous*. He shivers in the cold clammy dark. Coal dust glitters like jet in the light of his guttering candle. He sets the powder keg down carefully; its thirty-five brothers silently watch him from the shadows, half-shrouded in sheaves of firewood. But his hands are steady. His breathing is shallow. His heart remains firm.

The dirk hangs heavy from his hip, and his basket-hilted rapier scrapes the flagstones as he crab-scuttles to and fro, making the last final preparations. He's lit stores of gunpowder beneath a dozen castle strongholds in France, shattering great slabs of city wall into flying flint, left smoking ruins in his wake all across Flanders. This is a simple act of war – it should be second nature to him. Easier than breathing.

But he's not in Flanders. Not tonight.

And this isn't a castle.

The wide-brimmed hat is drooping over his eyes again; he sets it down. Straightens up.

And breathes out.

Months of planning and preparation, the murmurs buzzing in gloomy coffeehouses, gossip in smoky tavern backrooms spreading as easy as butter over hot bread. He's heard the whispers out of the North, the rumours that clotted and thickened like tar. Poor Margaret Clitherow who remained silent even as they heaped on more stones, higher and higher. All for the simple crime of sheltering the Lord's messengers under her roof. They were dragged out and soon swung from the noose themselves, poor wretches. Then their bellies carved open and their guts tugged out like lute strings. Disembowelled like hogs in the slaughterhouse. Other men and women were fed to the bonfires at Smithfield, refusing to recant their faith even as the flames licked higher. A thousand ghosts sigh over Smithfield and drift among the gallows of Tyburn Tree, wailing in the eternal fires of Purgatory ever since the king forbade proper funeral rites. The flames that eat through to the bone; old mothers and dead little babes bound in helpless agony, screaming for your prayers. Trapped in that barren charnel house with its flying cinders and sulphur reek, its yawning pits of boiling tar, its churning clouds of icy sheet.

What did James and his cronies *expect* after such harsh injustices – that they'd all roll over and submit?

And if they fail tonight . . .

He knows what horrific punishments await them. Everyone does. Their families stripped to penury by crippling fines. Their names cursed forever. The Tower's wicked instruments – the rack, the searing irons that tickle your feet. The thumbscrews. Their legacies trodden into the mud. Traitors to the crown. High treason's the gravest crime in the land – it's not like you're just stealing a neighbour's pig, is it?

Heavy boots on the stairs. He whirls around with a curse, scanning for an exit. None. Too soon, it's too soon!

Tramp tramp tramp.

He fumbles the candle free, jabs it onto the powder trail. It sparks instantly, fizzing across the flagstones.

A pang of regret gnaws his heart; his sister Ann sitting down to a family supper of ham and beans, his nieces Alice and Liz flicking spoonfuls of mashed potato about and giggling.

Tramp tramp tramp.

Alice, so fierce and wild, all scowls and scraped knees and tangled hair, swinging her doll like a morningstar when menaced with green vegetables. Liz, flame-haired blue-eyed Liz, who'd fling herself at him from around corners, clamber up him like the gnarled oak in their orchard and shriek with glee as they raced down the hall together. 'Faster, Uncle Guy, faster!' Grace, his ginger-furred princess, nuzzling into his hand and purring for her nightly saucer of milk, or dozing on his lap by the fireside, paws twitching as she dines on dream mice.

He'll never see them again . . .

Oh well. They'll remember him soon enough, after tonight.

Tramp tramp tramp. The scrape of pikes against stone, a jangle of heavy iron keys;

dancing yellow lantern light splashes into the vault. They flood down into the coal cellar, spreading out before him. Two. Five. Ten. A dozen torch-bearing guards sheathed in scarlet livery and grim steel, their halberd spikes and long swords glittering like icicles. He clenches his jaw and draws both blades, snorting like an old bull ringed by snarling dogs.

No fear. No retreat. No surrender. No quarter. He'll make them bleed, here deep in the bowels of Westminster.

C'mon, you pox-faced bucketheads . . . who's first?

He drops into a fighting crouch, naked steel gleaming in the torchlight. Behind him the powder hisses and flickers. Defend the fuse, come what may. Easy enough. He's always been an engineer, even when rising through the Spanish army. But every soldier knows the killing stroke.

The guards edge closer. He clashes his blades together, adrenaline coursing through him. They want to stem the march of history? They want to stop tonight from echoing down the ages?

Alone and outnumbered twelve to one, he bares his teeth.

They can bloody well *try*.

The guardsmen huddle around the guttering fireplace, nursing their beers. A hard, bloody night's work. Far away in the Tower, the intruder rots in a cell. A horrific plot foiled, peace restored once more, but the whispers still slither unchecked through the barracks: how he'd skewered Captain John Grant like a pig, leaving him squealing on the flagstones before whirling onto the others. Even after being disarmed by Will Baker, the man still managed to wrestle the corporal's sword off him and ring his helm like a bell before slashing his throat open. It had taken all ten remaining guards to bind him in chains, and still he'd fought like a snarling wolf, leaving two more wounded, Edward Lovatt with a broken arm, Rob Pryce with a smashed nose and poor young Tim Halleck missing an ear. Even after he'd lost both blades, the demon had fought with his fists, knees and elbows. When those were rendered useless, he'd used his teeth.

Owls wail outside. As London sleeps, the Yeomen of the Guard raise their tankards in a solemn toast: "to the plucky gent who fought."

When they finally wrench the rough hessian bag off his head, he's lost all track of time. He dimly recalls being roughly dragged along, buffeted, bruised and half-senseless as the blows rained down and their harsh snarls filled his ears. Shouting questions. Punching and kicking him. The raucous chatter of the guards and even their very stench, the onion stink of them, their gusts of beery breath as they manhandled him along gloomy passageways. Being bundled into a stone-cold damp room and shoved down into a hard wooden chair. A heavy oaken door slams shut. A key grates in the lock.

The flaring torchlight makes him flinch away. A bare, windowless room. A guard lurks by the torchlit door. Across the table opposite: a stern man in sombre black, with a steel-grey beard and a severe frown to match.

'My name is William Wade,' he says coldly. 'Lieutenant of the Tower. What is yours, sir?'

The lie spills easily from his lips. 'John Johnson.'

'Do you know why you are here?'

He stares blankly back, feigning dumb incomprehension. *Give the bastards nothing.*

'Very well . . . you are to be formally charged

with conspiracy to commit regicide against his majesty, wicked seditions and high treason,' Wade continues, his voice now tinged with malice, 'the penalty for which is a slow traitor's death on the scaffold.'

The strangling noose. The butcher's knife. Then the axe, the final sweeping wash of blood. What fun. He swallows.

'You have one chance, and one chance only, to prevent the awful fate that awaits you.' Wade taps the table. 'Give us the names of your companions, their numbers, their whereabouts. If your information leads to their capture, you will be immediately released forthwith from this hellhole. Do you understand what I'm telling you, sir?'

There it is. That thin meagre strand of hope that all prisoners cling to, the distant elusive promise of freedom.

His wrists are sore and chafed from the manacles. He stares down at his reddened flesh.

'You can return to your old life, sir,' Wade murmurs. 'All you have to do is cooperate.'

Cooperate. And go free.

What rot. As if he could ever believe them. As if they wouldn't string him up and hack him apart like a butchered pig as soon as he divulged everything he knew.

'Give us names,' Wade repeats.

He sucks in a ragged breath. Parts his cracked bloody lips.

'. . . John . . . Johnson.'

Wade's eyes widen. 'What?'

He slumps back in his chair, glaring defiantly. 'John Johnson.' The guard bristles and moves forward, hand drifting to his sword hilt.

Wade raises a hand. The guard stiffens, steps back.

Wade sighs and folds his arms, regarding him cooly. 'So it's like that, hmmm?'

He grins through bloody teeth. 'John . . .'

'Be quiet.'

'. . . Johnson.'

Wade's face hardens. 'Guard!' he barks.

The door bursts open and a trio of sword-drawn soldiers charge in.

'Let it be noted that due to the prisoner's hostile, provocative and uncooperative attitude, he is hereby sentenced to receive corrective punishment at sundown. In the form of twenty lashes.'

'Ooh,' he smirks. 'Watch me shiver.'

'Take him away!' Wade orders. 'Bind him in chains!' The four soldiers haul him upright and shove him towards the door, Wade's burning eyes following him. 'May the Lord have mercy on your soul. God save the king!'

He wrenches free. 'God *damn* the king!' he spits, before brawny arms envelop him and drag him bodily from the room.

'And gag him as well!'

Footsteps stamp down the corridor. Keys rattle in the lock. He braces himself. *Arrange your face. Never let them see you bleed.*

The cell door creaks open. The warder enters, approaches his cot and shakes his shoulder roughly. 'Rouse yourself. It's time.'

He rolls over, feigning a yawn. 'Already? Shame to awaken only to see your sorry mug. I was having such a wonderful dream.'

'Very funny,' the warder grunts. 'Come with us.' Behind him, a quartet of glowering guardsmen cluster in the doorway.

He straightens up on his cot. Smiles. 'I see. The royal escort, courtesy of the King. Good day, gentlemen. Doth my carriage await? To Westminster Hall to dine with the Archbishop, perhaps? Or maybe to Tower Hill to lop off my head.'

'It's the flogging frame fer you,' sneers a pox-scarred guard.

'Ah, yes. The frame. I *did* book that a while ago. I was beginning to fear my appointment would never come through.'

The warder bristles. 'You going to give us trouble?'

He shrugs. 'How the hell should I know? I've never been flogged before.'

The warder nods to the guards. 'Best clap the bracelets on him.' They clamp wrists already worn red by manacles. The warder slips a leather-wrapped length of dowel into his hand. 'Bite on this. Clamp down hard. It'll help. Somewhat.'

As he is frogmarched past other cells, unseen prisoners beat on their doors, roaring a crescendo of encouragement for him and curses for the Crown.

'Give 'em hell, son!'

'Don't let the bastards grind you down!'

'Fuck the King! A pox on his ministers!'

The tight huddle of men hurry up the stairs with Catholic taunts ringing in their ears.

Sunlight explodes in his face. He flinches, blinking hard like a mole roused from its burrow. Out in the chilly courtyard stand three men: the Lieutenant of the Tower, dressed with sober magnificence; a black-robed physician; a huge pink-faced man wearing a dark suit of fine quality. He looks like a prosperous city merchant.

A whip hangs from his meaty paw, from which dangle nine braided leather tails almost kissing the cobblestones. Each one is weighted with lead barbs to keep them from unravelling.

The lieutenant. The physician. The whip with its dangling tips of jagged metal.

This will be no ordinary flogging.

He clenches his jaw. Rough hands shove him forward to a timber flogging frame, with horizontal niches hewn at the waist and chest. His shirt is torn from his back and he's pressed into the frame angled forward, fettered by ankles and wrists. A leather collar is fastened around his neck to keep it from being broken. Bound like a pig for slaughter.

A hush has fallen over the courtyard. The air is still, the scene is one of theatrical reverence, even lurid religious spectacle. As if some twisted sacred ritual, sanctified by ancient law and primeval custom, is about to be enacted. Is Lieutenant Wade not master of the Tower, where his word is law, just as the King is overlord of England, and God the heavenly master of all?

The whipper bows to the lieutenant. In a sudden flurry he raises the whip high and slashes at the wall. Sparks fly. Mortar sprays from the masonry in a puff of dust.

The lieutenant steps back. Nods at the physician. 'Twenty lashes. Keep count, Master Dunlock.'

The prisoner breathes out.

'You may begin, Master Lynch.'

'One.'

Crack. Fingers of pink streak across his bared back. A shiver ripples through the watchers.

'Two.'

Crack. The colour deepens, broadening into thick crimson gashes. A moan bubbles up, rattling against clenched teeth . . .

He swallows it down.

Barely.

'Three . . . four . . . five . . .'

Where the lash strikes, the leaded tips are rolled by whipper Lynch so they rake across bare skin, curl and rip away flesh like shredded cabbage.

'Six . . . seven . . .'

He shudders. Tightens his fists. Lynch glistens with sweat, grunting as he throws his mighty bulk behind every vicious stroke.

'Nine . . . ten . . .'

Lynch pauses, gasping for breath as one of the tails snaps off, turns to the stand and selects another cat-o'-nine. While he does, the physician steps forward, stoops under the frame and peers up into the prisoner's face.

'Fuck off,' he snarls back.

'Continue, Master Lynch.'

Dunlock straightens up. 'The count was ten,' he calls. 'Eleven . . .'

The cobbles beneath him glisten with blood.

'Twelve . . . thirteen . . .'

He spits out the leather gag. 'Oh, they're hanging men and women for the trooping of the gold . . .'

'The hell's he doing?'

'I think ye might say he's singin', Sir Wade!'

'Well, Master Lynch, if you apply your strokes properly, he'll stop it.'

'Yessir!'

'And we'll keep up the fight until we're toothless, grey and old . . .'

'Fourteen . . . fifteen . . . sixteen . . .'

'They clap us in irons, hang us high,

What else must we do but fight and die . . .'

'Nineteen . . . twenty.'

A raw red tide has erupted, a massacre, a bloodbath of gore staining the cobblestones. The lieutenant snorts his displeasure; the whipper cringes, for his whipping days are numbered. The physician hastily feels for pulse, listens for heartbeat, prises open eyelids.

He smiles. Lets them unstrap him from the lashing post. Stands tall and faces them all, unbroken and unbowed.

'Keep your damn stretcher. I'll walk myself out.'

He tracks the slow crawling progression of time through his scant meals. Perhaps four, five days have gone by if he's correct about being fed twice every day. Eight o'clock and three o'clock, judging by the distant tolling church bells. The heavy metal door would creak open and the guards shove a tray into his cell. Sometimes it makes it in just fine. Sometimes it manages to spill out and slop all over the floor. It all depends on the sentry and his particular level of pettiness that day.

He doesn't know how long he's lain here. Hours? Days? Weeks? Just four stone walls. A bare stone shelf to sleep on, with not even a ragged blanket for bedding. A bucket that serves as a toilet, which no one bothers to empty until it was full. A rathole in the corner, where the sole other inhabitant of the cell emerges every night to scamper over his body in the dark, to gnaw at his threadbare hemp shirt while he sleeps.

The plate of slop they leave at his cell door remains untouched. Even the rat won't try it. He sleeps whenever he can, brief fitful snatches of unconscious his only escape, but always it seems that as soon as his eyelids droop shut, the cell door bangs open and he's hauled off for more.

Endless, endless questions. At any hour of the day or night the cell door crashes open, guards flood in and drag his limp body away for more questions, more beatings, more humiliations. And when he can't – or won't – answer, the gaolers manacle his wrists to a wall hook and drench him with buckets of icy water before dragging him, cold and shivering, back to his cell.

The rat comes and goes, providing the only entertainment he has, his only companion. Love-bites in the dark. *Is this all I have left? No lower to sink than a rat?*

And then the rat doesn't appear anymore. It's gone. And his loneliness is complete.

Torchlight flickers through the cell door outside, and sometimes it doesn't.

But the questions never stop.

If he talks, they will make the pain stop, they will make all of this torment stop. If he talks, they will feed him, clothe him, let him sleep. They won't hurt him anymore.

But if he talks, they'll win.

'I have been told to inform you,' the lieutenant begins, 'that you have been formally convicted by a special tribunal of terrorism and high treason, and that unless you are ready to offer full cooperation and name your comrades, you are to be executed on the gallows forthwith. Disembowelled like a pig for slaughter. Do you understand what I'm telling you? The severity of your punishment?'

'Yes,' he mutters.

Wade's eyebrows rise. 'So? Are you ready to cooperate?'

'No.'

In the hushed silence that follows, the tiniest hint of a smile flickers across his battered face.

Wade stares for a long minute, then sighs in weary exasperation. 'Very well.' He nods to the unseen guard behind. 'Escort Mister Johnson back to his cell. Arrange a detail of six men, then take him out behind the dog kennels and kill him.'

The guard leaves. Wade leans forward. 'All we want is one little piece of information,' he murmurs, showing the slightest touch of human warmth. As if, in the bitter end, he wants such a stubborn prisoner to survive, despite everything. 'Just give us something. *Anything.*'

He smiles back, a defiant glint in his eye. 'You're very kind . . . but I'd rather die behind the dog kennels, thanks.'

And something in Wade's face completely shuts down. A mask of grim resolve. 'You really have no fear anymore, do you?'

He shrugs. *What more could you possibly do to me?*

'Guard!' Wade barks. The cell door creaks open. 'Take the prisoner downstairs. And rack him.'

He glares mulishly back. 'I'll endure this too. Just you watch.'

Wade shakes his head. 'You won't.' His eyes are bleak with sad resignation. 'No one can withstand it. No one ever has. Everyone cracks on the rack.'

'I won't.'

'We'll see.'

'Do your worst,' he growls.

So they do.

Pain. Excruciating, blinding pain. He bites down the whimper that threatens to spill from bloody lips. His arms are burning. His legs afire with searing agony.

'It ends whenever you want it to,' Wade murmurs from above his head. 'Just give us their names. Tell us where they are.'

Don't say a word. Don't give them anything. Stay strong.

'I – don't – know,' he snarls.

Wade nods aside. The spindles turn. Ropes groan. Tighter. Tighter.

His bound limbs are stretched to breaking point. Tendons straining. Muscles tearing. Bones feathering toward the greenstick fractures that would come before the final, splintering breaks.

Deep inside, in some long-buried hidden vault of his heart, something cracks.

And at last – at long, long last – he begins to scream.

He betrayed them. He betrayed them all. He cracked open torn lips and their names dribbled out. Catesby. Winter. Percy. Wright. Once the words had begun, they spilled forth from his mouth like a dam crumbling. Dredged up from some deep well of despair inside.

'I'm here.'

He picks listlessly at a frayed thread on his sleeve. Catesby isn't here, he isn't real. He and his friends are far north, riding pell-mell through the Midlands gathering followers to their cause. Catesby uncurls from a patch of shadow, shuffles forward into the sliver of moonlight, a sad smile on that phantom face. He tears his gaze away, choked full of shame.

'After all this time, and you gave us up? Just like that?' Catesby snaps his fingers. Barks a harsh, bitter laugh. 'I'm not angry. I'm just . . . disappointed.' He sighs. 'We trusted you. And look how you repaid us. Traitor.'

He huddles into himself. When he forces himself to look up, Catesby is gone. Never was there.

The plate of cold gruel sits by the door. Blindly he crawls over and pulls the plate of slop towards himself. Scoops up handfuls of dripping mush and begins cramming them into his bloody mouth.

How far he has fallen! The lowest pit of degradation that he would even eat this vile filth. And yet here he is, his tears watering his wretched meal. Snuffling and weeping in the dark like a filthy animal.

It's what he deserves.

On the evening of 30th January, the lieutenant himself comes in. Says, 'Sir, it is the king's pleasure that you are to be executed tomorrow morning.'

So I won't live to see February, he thinks. Blackbirds jousting in the hedgerows, the cold evening dews after Michaelmas Day. Or the spring blossom, the snowdrops at dawn.

Wade fidgets with his plumed hat. Frowns at his boots. 'I recognise your dread. It afflicts many prisoners, in their last days alive upon this earth.'

'Is there a remedy?'

Perhaps no one has ever asked Wade this before. But he's a shrewd man, not one to mull things over. 'Accept your end. Do not shy away from it. Settle your mind. Make peace with yourself and God, sir.'

He looks up. 'I am still "sir"?'

Wade inclines his head gravely. 'You came in here as a gentleman, and you are to remain a gentleman unless I am instructed otherwise.'

His stern face softens; something thaws, deep in that wizened countenance. 'Despite your wicked intentions, sir, the king himself admires your fortitude. He applauds your resilience in the face of such' – he grimaces – '*persuasions*. As do we. Few prisoners have endured as long as you have. Rest assured, you have the king's utmost respect. If not his mercy.'

No, he concurs. *I thought not. Plotting to blow a man to hell does tend to colour his views.*

It is Monday evening.

Tuesday morning.

A prisoner facing his last day alive begins it as any other man – yawning, pissing, stretching, rubbing his prickly chin. Fed by constant river barges, the castle never sleeps; wagons rumble over the cobbles through the great gate.

Keys scrape in the lock. He brushes down his filthy shirt, squares his shoulders. The Chief Yeomen Warder stands in the cell doorway, resplendent in crimson and sable. Two uniformed warders behind, one bearing a pair of shears, the other a razor. The glint of steel sends a shiver through him. *They mean to shave me bald. Another petty humiliation, to parade me through the streets like any common pickpocket headed for the gallows.* But he won't give them the pleasure of hearing him beg. *I am a Northman, a soldier, a dutiful brother and loving son. I can manage a damn haircut. And besides, it always grows back.*

'You must be shorn,' grunts the chief warder.

Like a sheep, he thinks, *stripped naked for harvest.* He raises his chin proudly.

'Get on with it, then,' he snarls.

The elder guard takes up the shears. He sits still as stone as the shears click and snip, and the

108

blades whisper over his scalp. Drifts of dark hair tumble to the flagstones, unwashed and matted with blood. When his curls are scattered around his feet, the younger guard begins scrapping away the ragged stubble with his razor. A fresh jab of pain as the blade nicks his skin. Warm blood trickles past his ear. He dimly remembers all the times his mother had cradled him in her tender arms, kissing away his aching bruises from another schoolyard brawl. Her kisses were always warm. But the razor is ice-cold.

The chief warder steps back and casts an appraising eye over him. 'Very good. Now clothe him.'

The others hesitate. 'Really, sir?' mutters the younger warder. 'He ain't worth 'em.'

'He's still a gentleman,' growls the chief warder. 'And a gentleman deserves his final dignity. Clothe him.'

The breeches are far too large for him; they sag off his bony hips. The shirt has a large gash down the left sleeve. They're filthy with dried mud.

But they'll do.

Dressed like a pauper. A bark of laughter

109

bursts from his lips, bleak and bitter.

'Find this funny, do yer?' scowls a guard. 'You'll soon be screamin' in Hell.'

Maybe, he thinks, *but I'll see you there too having your tongue ripped out with red-hot pincers. And that'll be hilarious.*

He stifles another yawn. But reminds himself: you must not look tired, or weary, or broken, or an inconsolable wretch overcome with grief. If a man should live as if every day is his last, he should also die cheerfully; as if there is a day still to come, and yet another after that. As if he's just stepping out for a brisk walk, stretching his legs before another beautiful dawn. *I am leaving this damp putrid cell for the last time. I won't be coming back.*

A bell begins to toll. His long imprisonment is at an end. He turns from his escort, raises his head high. 'Let's go, then. Haven't got all day.' The scaffold awaits him across the city. The sooner he sets off, the sooner he will see it.

He emerges blinking at the searing sunlight like a drowsy mole awakened from its burrow. Before the yawning portcullis, two dozen guardsmen in crimson await him, surrounding a horse-drawn wattle hurdle. Their helms and steel

110

breastplates gleam in the sunlight, but their eyes are hard shards of flint, cold and merciless.

He stares, amazed, at the bristling ranks of his escort. *All these? For me?*

Their captain steps forward. 'Sir, I am Sir John Forley. His Majesty has given me command of your escort. Rest assured, my men and I will see you safely through the streets.'

He returns the man's nod. 'Sir John. Am I to die alone today?'

Forley shakes his head. 'Thankfully not, sir. We have already conveyed Thomas Winter, Robert Keyes and Ambrose Rookwood earlier. They await you at the scaffold.'

So I will die alongside friends, he thinks, with a flush of warm relief. *That's something*. Ravens swirl over St Thomas's Tower like windblown scraps of black cloth. Their harsh clamour echoes across the courtyard.

He descents the steps on trembling legs. He had come to London in fine clothes, riding a fine horse. He is leaving bald and bedraggled, caked in mud and blood. *But I'm leaving. And that's all that matters.*

He smiles at the wicker panel of twisted saplings awaiting him. 'And is this to be my fine carriage for today? You're too kind.'

John nods gravely. 'By your leave, sir. A regrettable formality. There are precedents to be observed.' They unlock his shackles, push him face-down onto the wooden hurdle and rebind his chaffed wrists and ankles. Cruel cords cut deep into his skin, spreadeagled, almost kissing the cobbles.

They will walk out of the fortress and turn northward to Tower Hill, to the public scaffold that awaits all condemned traitors. A short journey. Two hundred yards, at most. All over in a heartbeat.

On the scaffold he will praise the king: his loving mercy (ha!), his grace, his care for all (most of) his subjects. It is expected of him, and he has a duty to the family he leaves behind. Before he is half-hanged, castrated and then slowly – leisurely – gutted by the executioner, he will tell the crowd: I am not a heretic, I am no traitor, I die a member of our all-loving church, and make of that whatever you will.

The captain turns, raises a gloved hand. 'Walk on!' Someone smacks the horse's rump, and with a jolt they move off. They pass under the towering gatehouse out into the open air, turn left along the wharf towards Tower Street. The sunlight is blinding; to his right the Thames glitters like burnished gold. The morning air is thick with the old familiar stinks of London. Sour wine, bread baking, rotting fish and nightsoil, smoke and sweat and horse piss. The fortress bells are ringing, summoning the city to bear witness to his punishment. The cobbled wharf is swarming with jeering onlookers, but as his procession approaches a sudden silence falls.

Captain Forley steps forward, addressing the seething mob. 'Behold a sinner before you!' he calls. 'For he has committed treasonous crimes. He has confessed his monstrous sins, and now comes before you with a humbled heart, stripped of all secrets and pride, bared before gods and men to make his final march of penitence.'

'Traitor!' roars a butcher, his apron red with gore. Growls ripple through the crowd.

A gust of icy wind makes him shudder, gooseprickles rising along his arms and legs. His fingers tighten into fists, nails digging into his palms. *I am a soldier. A wolf of the north. I will not cringe for them.* They are looking at him, all the hungry eyes. *I have sinned and must atone, must parade my shame before every beggar in this stinking city. They think this will break my spirit, unman me before the scaffold, but they are wrong.* For what are they seeing? *Just a man*, he reminds himself, *and even one man alone can accomplish wonders*. His escort fan out ahead of him, the guardsmen shoving men aside to forge a path through the leering crowd.

It seems to take forever to cross the fortress wharf, but finally paved cobblestones give way to muddy track beneath him. The stern bastions of the Tower loom overhead. They're swallowed in shade once more, and he shivers at the sudden chill.

'Bastard!' a woman hisses.

He ignores her. Rests his cheek against the hurdle's twisted wood. *There will be far more insults, and far worse. These creatures have no sweeter joy in life than jeering at the condemned*. He could not silence them, so he must pretend he cannot hear them. He will not see them either, will keep his head high, eyes fixed on Tower Hill ahead. He will find his salvation there, soon enough.

The absurdity almost makes him smile: when he soon lies dead and the hangman begins wielding his butcher's knife in ghastly earnest, other people will be having utterly boring mornings. It will be approaching lunchtime, there will be stewpots bubbling, meat sizzling, ladles clattering, a hundred cats mewing for milk, a hundred dogs whining for table scraps. While he meets his grisly fate, napkins will be unfurled, fingers dipped in rosewater, graces murmured, bread broken. And when the crumbs are finally swept away and the pots piled high for scouring, his body will be broken meat for crows while the executioner cleans his gory blade.

We are all dying eventually, just at different speeds. The crowd surging alongside him toward the execution ground are trampling over their own dead forefathers and mothers. They say the bones of untold thousands lie scattered deep underground. When the black shadow of plague stretched over these rooftops, clawing at every shuttered window and crawling underneath every bolted door, Londoners were felled in such swarms and carted off in such hurry that they were buried still in their good boots; a hundred thousand skeletons rattle under London's pavements, a generation of clothed cadavers underfoot with not even their purses cut. If any brave man dares dig for it, there's a vast fortune awaiting beneath our feet.

The hurdle lurches left. He raises his head, unease churning through him. Surely a mistake . . . no. They are turning left, not right towards Tower Hill, his guards closing up behind him. The horse continues its same plodding pace onward, steered firmly by the bridle.

He looks back. Tower Hill slowly recedes into the distance. No scaffold upon its summit. 'Wait. Where are we –'

'Didn't you know?' a guard sniggers. 'We're headed for Parliament. The scene of your crimes.'

He slumps his head onto the wattle with a groan, rough bark digging into his cheek. The long march, then. Three miles. A drawn-out spectacle for the dregs of Eastcheap and Fleet Street.

Another guard smirks down at him. 'We're taking you to Westminster Palace Yard. You'll die before the very building you failed to destroy.'

That's right, he thinks bitterly. *Pour salt on the wound, why don't you. Go on. Rub it right in. Bastard.*

How many times could he have turned back,

said no, walked away, altered his destiny? The plot would never have been born, but his friends would still be alive. Raising their families. Living out their days. *I would have found Alice a good match. Walked her down the aisle one proud day. I should have stayed in York, picking apples and helping Anne feed the chickens. I could have ended my days safe in my own bed, surrounded by my loving family. Held my nieces' hands for the last time.*

Would have. Should have. Could have.

Didn't.

Instead he had ridden south to London with murder on his mind. Had broken bread with plotters and renegades. And after that there was no turning back.

The memories seem so distant now. Catesby is dead, and all his companions up north shredded by lead, minced by steel. Even his own father is long gone. And here he lies, dragged through Eastcheap behind a horse's arse, under the eyes of a hungry mob. No others will be dragged with him today. This ordeal is his to bear, and his alone.

But at least I won't die lonely. Small victories.

Shops and timbered houses close in all around

them as they begin their march along Eastcheap. The going is slower here; the filthy lane is narrow, the masses jammed tightly together, surging back and forth like a raging tide. His guards clear a path ahead, forcing the crowd back with staves and spearbutts. A tradesman curses as the soldiers haul his cart aside, spilled cabbages tumbling into the muck.

He looks behind him. He can still see the domed towers and crenelated walls of the White Keep, its looming silhouette blocking out the sun. Dismay shudders through him. *Have I really only come such a short distance?*

The streets are as crowded as any market day. Everywhere he looks he sees ravenous eyes. Men and women. Some have children perched on their shoulders, gawping at him. Beggars and thieves, tradesfolk and tanners, stableboys and butchers; all the filthy unshaven scum have come out to see a proud man brought low. Soldiers clear a path ahead, forcing the crowd back with staves. But there's no hurry. They will continue onward at the same plodding, sedate walking pace, until he reaches his final reckoning at Westminster.

Soon the street widens out onto the open plaza before St. Paul's Cross, the vast cathedral soaring before him. His escort fans out ahead, shoving at those blocking the way while more soldiers fall in alongside. The muffled dullness of the horse's hooves become sharper and crisper, ringing out as they cross the paved square. *Clip clop. Clip clop.*

Scowling faces everywhere, a seething mass of frothing flesh. And gazing down upon them all, the other Londoners of lichened stone and rusting metal, those frozen monsters sneering and sniggering above the populace, fanged rabbits and winged serpents, grimacing leather-winged imps and snarling dragons, horned devils dancing on cloven hooves or cramming babes into their gaping maws, all gobbled up except their helpless flailing feet; limestone or leaden, marbled and metalled; bulbous-eyed gargoyles shrieking and gurning and retching from buttresses, flowered spires and rooftops.

'Traitor!' a woman screams. Something flies out of the crowd. Some rotted vegetable. Brown and slimy, it splatters across his forehead. *I am not afraid. I am a soldier.*

He raises his head. Somewhere far ahead, out across the slow curve of the river, beyond this snarling sea of hungry eyes and gaping mouths

119

and dirty faces, the Palace of Westminster awaits him.

Cold mush oozes down his cheeks. Dripping into his eyes. 'Hot pies,' sings a baker's boy. 'Getcha hot pies here!' The guardsmen force a path ahead, shoving men aside with their spears, clearing a narrow path. *Clip clop. Clip clop.* Every step brings Westminster Hall nearer. Every step brings him that much closer to his gristly end. His salvation.

A shrill whistle from above. A woman leans out of an overhanging window, hefting a large bucket. 'A drink for the thirsty rogue!' she cackles. 'Quench yer thirst on this!'

And heaves out the contents.

Foul stinking urine splashes over them, spattering the horse's rump and drenching him to the bone. The horse shrieks and flinches away. The men-at-arms curse and shake their fists upward, but the surrounding crowd cheers. The empty bucket clatters to the ground.

When he reopens his eyes, spluttering and dry-heaving, they're hemmed in on all sides by a jeering crush of spectators. Worse, a hundred times worse, he has lost all sight of the river, of Westminster Hall. It's hidden now, walled off from his gaze by the tall timbered buildings to either side. 'Where . . . where are we?'

Forley pats his shoulder. 'Just ahead, sir. Through Lud Gate, then out along Fleet Street and we're there.' The horse is snorting and stamping while its handler soothes it, tenderly stroking its nose and crooning into its face. They march on.

The shouting seems much louder here than back on Tower Street, perhaps because the mob is crowding so much closer. 'Traitor' and 'bastard' are most common, mingled with 'Papist cunt' and 'sinner'. *What wonderful civilised folks Londoners are*, he thinks. *So refined. So benign. So genteel.* Now and again he hears someone drunkenly bawl 'Long live the king!' and a dozen throats echo it back. The lane underfoot is filthy as he scrapes along, his frame trailing through puddles and spattering his legs. *No one's ever died of wet feet before*, he tells himself. *It's only rainwater. Not horse piss.*

But more filthy refuse showers down from windows and balconies overhead: rotten fruit, pails of nightsoil, eggs that explode into sulphurous stink when they splatter onto the ground.

The stern ramparts of Lud Gate loom ahead, flanked by the crumbling ruins of the old Roman wall. They pass under the wide shadowed archway of Lud Gate and emerge into glaring sunshine, the broad thoroughfare of Fleet Street stretched before them. And he almost laughs with relief. For ahead, spread out along the northern bank of the Thames, are the sprawling cattle pens and stockyards of Smithfield meat market. The mournful lowing of thousands of terrified bullocks fills the air, great herds awaiting their grim slaughterhouse fate under the butcher's axe, his meathooks, his knives. The foul stench of manure and bloody tripe fills the air. The endless buzz of a million droning flies.

And beyond them clear as day, out across the wide southward curve of the river, rises the imposing mass of Westminster Hall. Its gilded towers blush pink in the rising dawn. *We made it out. There lies my end.* Never has the stink of offal and dung smelled so sweet. *It's not so far now.* Once they reached it, the worst of his torment would soon be over. He will see his father again. *Edward is waiting for me. My beloved father. I can do this for him. I must.*

He sees the dead cat far too late. Limbs

flailing, its carcass sails over the heads of his guards, smashes onto the cobbles and bursts open at his feet, spattering his legs with entrails and crawling maggots. A ragged laugh ripples through the crowd.

He ignores it. *I am blind and deaf, and they are but worms*, he tells himself. *Easy for them to taunt a bound man broken from the rack.* 'Traitor, traitor,' chants a fishwife. Somewhere to the right another voice sings counterpoint to hers, some street hawker shouting 'Chestnuts, hot chestnuts here!' A wailing gull wheels overhead. 'Papist prick,' a drunkard roars from a high window, raising his tankard in a mocking toast. 'All hail the Papist prick!' All around him is a babble of scornful noise. *Words, just useless words pissing in the wind*, he thinks. *Sticks and stones may break my bones, but names will never hurt me.*

Familiar faces swim out of the crowd. A young bearded man peers down from a window with Catesby's stern frown, so alike that he gasps and wrenches his gaze away. A woman shoves forward through the seething throng, glaring at him with Anne's accusing brown eyes. 'Bastard!' she snarls.

There's something prickling his eyes, stinging, blurring his sight. He cannot cry, he must not, these worms must never see him weep. His girls are not here, they are all far away, safe in the north.

And then he sees Liz, his darling Liz, his sweet laughing niece with her fiery curls, now leering with the rest, her ice-blue eyes burning with vicious malice . . .

And there is no stopping the tears. They burn down his cheeks like acid. 'Yah, look at him blubber!' hoots a gleeful stallholder.

'Please,' he mumbles to the shit-smeared cobblestones. 'God forgive me. I confessed.'

Forley squeezes his shoulder. 'You did, sirrah. And this is your punishment.' He points ahead. 'It is not much farther now, see? Down the street, that's all.'

He raises his tear-stained face. *Down the street. That's all.* It's true. Crimson stonework looms. They are passing the corner of King Street; the rosy-brick ramparts of the Holbein Gate tower on his right, the palace of Whitehall sprawled beyond it. Ahead rises the high vaulted chamber of Westminster Hall. Mockingly untouched. *Look at us*, its distant ornate spires seem to taunt him. *Thirty-six barrels of prime gunpowder, and you never touched us. Pathetic. Not even a measly scratch to show for it.*

'Papist,' someone screeches.

'Shame,' crows another woman. 'Shame! Shame!' It does not matter now. He is almost home.

The crowd thickens ahead, pushing forward with hungry eyes. 'Make way!' call his escort, forging a path with fists and staves. 'Make way!'

If anything, the jeers and shouts are cruder here, even under the hallowed eyes of saintly statues. His long journey has not passed south of the Thames, so all the denizens of Southwark and Lambeth are packed through the Strand to better see the show. The faces leering at him from behind the guardsmen's spears seem twisted, monstrous, hideous, a hissing, spitting, jabbering swarm of beasts. Pigs and ragged children run amok, crippled beggars and cutpurses swarm like roaches through the packed throng. Men with festering facial sores weeping yellow pus, wizened hags with drooping dugs and rotten brown teeth, a smirking rouge-lipped whore stroking a huge snake draped over her shoulders. They all grin and lick their lips and hoot as he is dragged by, hurling obscene insults and mockery. *Words are wind*, he thinks, *words cannot hurt me. I am a soldier. I was loyal. I am brave.*

He does not feel brave, though. He feels filthy, used, broken, discarded. The piss has soaked right through his sodden shirt now, and his aching wounds begin to sting. Bloody, battered and bound, he is only a man, another pathetic nobody scorned before the mob.

A fresh stench fills his nose: the foul reek of burning meat. And suddenly they are at the foot of the scaffold. Before him, high above, the bodies of Winter and Keyes swing limply in the breeze. Rookwood's disembowelled corpse is sprawled atop a bloodstained trestle table below, his organs hissing and sizzling in a brazier like so much butcher's tripe. As he watches, the black-hooded executioner steps forward, reaches deep inside Rookwood's gaping chest, and pulls out a coil of slimy pink intestine. A fresh wave of cheers from the crowd.

A thousand hungry eyes watch him limp towards the scaffold, under the leering skulls of long-dead traitors. He sweeps by them, never looking up. Can feel their eyeless gaze upon him. *Remember us*, they seem to plead, *remember us hereafter.* Within their carved limestone niches, the saints seem to watch as well.

At the foot of the scaffold he crumples. Doubles up screaming as violent pain rips through his body. The jeers redouble. He claws his way upright, gripping the banister with white-knuckled fingers.

The ladder looms above him. *It's ten short steps,* he tells himself. *Like any tall staircase. Get moving.*

He breathes out. Gathers his courage.

And starts to climb.

The hangman's noose slips around his neck, gentle as any woman's loving embrace.

They mean to strangle me slow. Cut me down alive and rip me apart like any common steer. For the crowd's sick entertainment.

Not if I can help it. I am the captain of my own fate. I am the master of my soul. They want me to go out on their terms? I'll go out on my own.

With a prayer on his lips and joy singing in his heart, Guy Fawkes leaps from the ladder into the fractured sky.

GRAVEDIGGER

Ninepence per body. Not bad pay, if you're brave enough.

Or desperate enough.

'Slowin' down, eh, mate?'

Will swats my arm, grinning. 'Piss off.'

A cloth bound across the mouth, thick leather gloves and a long-sleeved shirt, and you're good to go. It rained last night; we slip and squelch through our gruesome task. Me, Will Caxton, Jack Brook, Tom Weaver and a half-dozen others. Three cartloads of lolling corpses behind us, a bleak expanse of churned earth before our eyes. Charterhouse ought to be bustling at this hour: the smell of roasted meat wafting over from Smithfield market, the playful chime of the priory bells.

Not today. The air is silent as the yawning pit that stretches before us, a deep, dark gash into the earth, as if made by the careless slash of a giant claw. Nothing but the wet crunch of shovels biting through the slimy earth, sinking deeper, deeper. A dull curse as Will slips in the mud, a muffled cough. No birds call; even the flies keep their wary distance as we dig. The air feels cloying and heavy, as if the whole city holds its breath. Tom leans back on his spade, mops his brow with a gloved hand. Our shirts are soaked in sweat; smells revolting, but better safe than sorry. Another burial crew over in St Giles worked stripped to the waist. Morons. Half of them feverish by sunset, the other half dead within the week. Mayor's orders. Shirts on all throughout the day, no matter the sweltering heat. No exceptions.

We knew when the rumours first shivered through the streets of Blackfriars, as relentless as the cartloads of dead pouring in from the countryside. How could they not spread? Panic always wins. Whole households stripped to the bone. A sickness that slaughtered in a mere morning, they said: merry at breakfast, dead by noon.

Not everyone fears it, though. Always some who find a way to twist tragedy into perverse opportunity. Gossiping washerwomen chattered about lucky charms and infusions; over at St Bartholomew, Friar Moreland did a roaring street trade in holy medals and sacred relics. Hollow-cheeked and lean as a gnawed cutlet, he'd bellow his oaths over the clamour of the bells, passing out wood shavings to desperate clutching hands. 'Behold a piece of the True Cross! Protect your souls from harm! Only ten shillings!' Christ must have been crucified four times over, at the rate that snake was forking them out.

The Great Pestilence. Fear, panic and despair. Some people even made a killing from it. (Heh! See what I did there?)

And on we'd march, tramping from street to street, to every household with a blood-red cross daubed on the door and a watchmen lurking outside. Young, old . . . it made no difference. Men, women, children. Twelve under one roof in Aldgate, stiff and silent beneath the eaves. Two girls tucked into bed side by side, their stern little faces relaxed into sweetness.

Two hours since we began, slowly sinking into the earth as the voiceless skeletons clamoured around us, reaching out with bare-boned fingers. Eight metres. Ten. Our orders were simple: find room for fresh arrivals. Once you can't, then make more. The reigning dead reduced to splintered shards, chalk-white fragments, as if our toil had churned them like dry bread in an old man's mouth. All around us rises the sickening reek of grave mould, the cloying overripe stench of decay. Every second thrust of the spade levers out some ghastly revelation. A jawbone with three gleaming molars. A gaping skull, spiders weaving their webs across lidless rotten eye sockets. The pale curve of ribs, like the staves of an old barrel. A noseless face crawling with maggots. The delicate filigree of a hand. Some with ragged tatters of clothing still clinging to yellowing bones, their arms merely hanging threads of rotting grey flesh.

We toil on, serenaded by that dull chorus of blade on soil, the bones clacking together like ale pots. Jack gently prises one of the smaller skulls from its earthly cradle, wipes a smear of mud from its brow and settles it again, like a fledgeling returned to its rightful nest. The dead are no longer surprised to see us – where once even the barest bones seemed affronted, cowed like some shy person pushed naked into the leering street, now they lie passive as brides awaiting the hands of the gravediggers to carry them up into the sunlight. It almost makes me grin; the gone-ahead, the passed-over lifted from crushing darkness by bearded angels smoking clay pipes!

It's nauseating work, sure. But it pays well. Every sunset our purses grow heavier with sterile coins washed in vinegar, fat brown pennies that we hoard like precious jewels. Our daily keep in bread and soup.

And beer, of course. The harder the day, the more strong grog needed to endure it. Today is a three-bottle day. A tenth of a bottle per man per metre dug. Is that the calculation? Not something they teach you in school.

Maybe I'll try being a rat-catcher. If I survive the week, God willing.

Besides bones, other things are uncovered and passed up. A deformed metal cross, greenish. A broken broach in the shape of a rose. Buttons. An antique-looking belt buckle. A rusty knife blade. Nothing of value yet. And if something valuable should be found? Who then is the legal owner? The corpse it was lifted from? The gravedigger who uncovered it? Perhaps the Lord Mayor. He pays us, after all.

The dull thump of metal on wood. Will and Tom slither down into the pit to scrape away the earth. A huge coffin emerges. Too heavy to lift. They lever their spades beneath the lid, peel it open like an oyster.

And stagger back, aghast. 'Jesus wept!' We stare down.

Inside the coffin lie two men, entwined together in a tender embrace. Curled periwigs, powdered white skin, rouge-red lips, fingernails, *eyelashes*. Perfectly preserved, right down to the black beauty spot on one's cheek, the luxuriant drooping brown moustache of the other. Both bodies have been mummified like dried flowers; even their thin woollen shroud only needs some washing to restore it. A final dying wish, no doubt a hefty bribe slipped to the vicar to turn a blind eye. Together in death forevermore.

Jack crosses himself. 'Bloody hell.' We exchange uneasy glances; burying tattered skeletons and maggot-ridden corpses is one thing, but men lying as if peacefully asleep,

133

wrapped in each other's arms like illicit lovers? We hesitate – buggery's a hanging offence, a grievous sin, but . . . it's wrong to disturb them, somehow. Improper.

Clattering hooves; a cloaked rider thunders towards us out of the dusty haze. The fearsome pale mask of the plague doctor in his dark oilskin overcoat. I shiver as those blank sightless eyes slide over me. A horrifying monster, a ghastly creature vomited from a nightmare, from the depths of Hell, from Satan himself. He towers over us, cloaked all in black; the hideous cruel beak in place of a mouth, curved like that of a giant predatory bird. Hungry for carrion.

He dismounts and approaches us, his mask sweeping over the earth vomiting up its howling dead even as we shovel more into unhallowed ground.

'Finished, have you?' That harsh grating voice. It can't be . . .

Jack glowers. 'Aye, sir.'

The cloaked figure saunters over to peer into the depths. Lifts his mask with a gloved paw.

I clench my fists.

The pockmarked face of Squire John Hackett. Taxman and bogeyman in equal measure. Cursed in every Cheapside tavern and mocked in every Southwark market. A conniving rat bastard leaching honest folk of their hard-earned riches. Half the men here owe him rent, the other half want to beat his brains out if given the chance.

His lip curls. 'Where d'you find these sodomites? Why ain't they burning already?'

Tom shuffles forward. 'Didn't seem proper, sir,' he mumbles.

Hackett sniggers. 'They're painted fops who value lip-paint more than manhood. Flies in the face of natural law. Burn 'em along with the cattle. All they're good for.'

Tom hesitates. 'But sir –'

Hackett bristles. 'Mind your tongue! They're soiling the resting places of good honest Englishmen. Do as I say!'

We close ranks, resentment crackling in the air. It's a desolate wasteland, a muddy field strewn with corpses, but to us this is sacred ground, sacrosanct only to the dead and those who lay them to rest.

And he's trespassing.

Will's voice breaks the hushed silence. 'No.'

Hackett rounds on him, seething. 'Damn yer eyes! Didn't you hear me? That's an order! Want to be thrown in the stocks?'

Will throws down the shovel with a clatter and steps towards him. Hackett's eyes dart around at a wall of stony faces.

Jack lifts his pickaxe.

Hadn't grabbed it for nothing.

And Tom Weaver, for all his clumsy lolloping slowness, has understood. He approaches like a great lumbering bear, gnarled hands on broad hips. Solidly built. Impossible to knock over. Strong as an ox.

Hackett flinches, glances around for an escape. None.

Will leans in. 'You liddle worm,' he growls. 'Just say one more word against 'em, you bloodsucker, and you'll be screaming in hell.'

Hackett shrinks back, gulping like a stranded fish. 'S-steady now, gents! What's it to you? They're only painted buggers –'

I feel the jarring crunch all the way to my elbows. A beautiful scything swing flooded with boiling rage, two hundred pounds of sizzling fury in a vicious crashing two-handed blow. The wet crunch of bone; Hackett flops into the mud in a sprawled tangle of limbs.

No one breathes. We are stricken with dread,

all of us. Fear sinks its talons into our bones; whatever will we tell the constables? Our friends? Our loved ones?

Then Will slithers down into the hole, looks up at us. 'C'mon, you lazy bastards! Who's gunna help me?'

A moment's hesitation: then we clamber down after him and bend to our task once more, shovels gouging into the earth. Deeper. Deeper. Hackett's body slowly vanishes as clods of soil splash over him. Legs first, then the torso. Finally the face.

Ten metres of grave dirt. Deep enough for anyone. Just another forgotten soul buried deep beneath God's earth, awaiting the worms. Unmarked and unmourned.

Good riddance, I think.

We close the men's coffin and return them to their final resting place, almost reverential. The other bodies soon join them, gently laid side by side as if peacefully asleep. Closer to heaven, maybe? We're not sure. But it feels right.

The sun kisses the horizon as the last shovelful of soil tumbles into the pit. We climb out and gather at the edge, each lost in his own thoughts. Three cartloads of rotting dead consigned to the earth, three dozen angels and one devil entombed together . . .

Then Will chuckles, claps me on the back. 'A good day's work, mate! First round's on me tonight!'

We trudge away, a tired company of soldiers leaving a hard-won battlefield, shovels and mattocks draped over our shoulders like muskets. The stink of putrefaction clinging to our boots.

Plague, desolation, misery. Play your cards right, and you might just make a killing from it.

Just ask us. We'd know.

OATHBREAKER

I can still hear their screams at night. Haunting my darkest nightmares. I did what had to be done. I was a soldier. Good at fighting. Good at killing, too. Never disobeyed an order. Never threw down my musket in disgust. My sergeant's sword gleamed proudly on my hip. Steadfast and loyal, that's me. They were traitors, after all. Betrayed King William, their rightful ruler. Spurned his mercy. Too proud to declare their allegiance when he demanded their fealty. Those Highlanders deserved their grim fate.

But I'll never forget the screams. They'll haunt me until my dying day. And I deserve it.

The trick was to get it over with, then drive it clean out of your mind. To tell yourself: these aren't people. These aren't innocents. These are MacDonalds.

War hardens a man, and after a few years in the army he can stomach almost anything. Good soldiers follow orders. Obey their officer's commands unflinchingly, without question. Even so, it's a lot to ask of a man – to eat another man's food, to share the warmth of his fireside, to sleep soundly under his roof, accept his hospitality . . . and then murder him in his sleep.

Still, King William was determined to be rid of the "Auld Fox" MacIain and the rest of his bothersome MacDonald clan once and for all. So we were billeted on them, with the excuse that Fort William was far too overcrowded to hold us. As we marched into the frozen glen – a hundred and twenty redcoats of the Earl of Argyll's Regiment – MacIain's sons melted out of the mist before us, their swords drawn. The tallest stepped forward and raised his hand.

'Come ye as friends or foes?' he called.

'As friends,' Captain Robert Campbell of Glenlyon answered, his smile as cold as midwinter ice. 'Just friends.'

For twelve days we shared their poor wee houses in that great valley of Glencoe, where a river of wind flows always cold and where the snowcapped mountains tower high into the sky. The Master of Stair had said it must be done in wintertime, the one time of year the Highlanders could not elude us and carry their wives, children and cattle off into the surrounding mountains.

They didn't suspect a thing. After all, we had accepted MacIain's hospitality, and that should have guaranteed our goodwill even though we were Campbells. (Campbells and MacDonalds had been at each other's throats for decades of long enmity; that's why Stair chose us for the job.) The sacred unwritten law of the Highlands had eased their suspicions – they thought they had nothing to fear.

So we played cards with the MacDonalds, drank with them, swapped stories around their smouldering peat fires. We sat down to supper cooked by their women, and our knuckles brushed theirs as we reached into the same bread bowl for food. The children tugged at our uniforms, pleading to be sung a song. Their mothers hushed them away to bed: 'Dinnae fash the officer: he needs his sleep.' The old wrinkled

141

matriarch bustled between us, doling out stew and cooing over our crimson tunics. 'Look at these fine soldiers,' she chuckled to the two ragged waifs clinging to her skirts. 'Bravest boys I've ever seen. God bless ye!' It's a good thing the firelight had guttered low and we were still wearing our wide-brimmed tricorns, for none of us could bear to look her in the eye.

When her death came, I hope it was quick. She'd earned that much, at least.

At nightfall we were summoned outside and given our strict orders by Campbell. No bed-rest tonight. When they saw us checking our muskets and fixing bayonets the MacIain brothers frowned.

'What's happening?' the eldest asked, eyes narrowed in suspicion.

Campbell just laughed. 'Local band of robbers in the next valley. Dumb sheep-stealers. We'll go after them early tomorrow.'

The time was set for five in the morning, when the clansmen would still be fast asleep or just stirring. All night long we waited, watching the moon drift over the glen through tangles of snow-cloud, a thistledown of snow falling. By three o'clock it had thickened into a blizzard.

Our tunics were drenched in cold.

What I remember most about that fateful night was . . . just how quiet it was. During the waning hours of starlight, it was a silent wait. We all knew what was about to happen, what evil we were about to do. The bayonet's an ugly, primitive weapon. A glorified spear, nothing more. Up close and personal. Did we have any hidden doubts among our ranks? Any private, traitorous thoughts? Guilt? Remorse? Perhaps, but no one ever said a word. Not during that last supper huddled around smoky firesides, not during the long watchful hours under chilly stars, and not when the first streak of dawn glowed on the eastern horizon, a faint slash of crimson. Not a word. Until Campbell mounted his horse, glanced at his pocket-watch and drew his claymore. An ugly, brutish weapon. He turned to us with a curt nod: 'Five o'clock, lads. Let's go to work.'

And so we did.

Bayonets fixed. Marching through the snow under the eaves. Swallowed in shadow. Huddled forms around guttering embers. Pick your target. Like skewering a pig. In, grunt. Out, grunt. No shots to be fired, that was the order. But some of us were jumpy – or squeamish – and we used our guns. The MacDonalds would have woken anyway. The screaming would have woken them soon enough.

We killed more than thirty. You wouldn't think that would take long. And yet the screaming seemed to last for an eternity. Sometimes I still hear it in my dreams. Men, women, children. Everyone under seventy, the order had said, and don't bother the Governor with prisoners. They streamed out of their hovels and turned to run. But we were waiting. Campbell spurred his horse after a knot of fleeing shadows, hacking them down with his sword. A child stumbled and fell. The horse thundered over it. Campbell laughed.

I wrenched my gaze away.

No mercy. If they barred the doors against us, we set the house alight and burned it down, with them all inside. Women. Children.

Thirteen in one hut.

In the confusion some got away, out of the village and away into the night. Didn't matter. It's so cold up there, with the snowdrifts so deep, and only their thin nightshirts for sleeping, barefoot, without cloak or blanket; we knew they'd soon freeze to death out on the pitiless mountainsides.

In the hovel where I had slept, nine clansmen were huddled around the morning firepit when we went in shooting. Four died where they sat. We split up and went after the women, the bairns, the old folk. They wept, they cursed and pleaded . . . but our bayonets were deaf. I came face-to-face with the owner, whose knuckles had brushed mine as I reached out for bread at supper. Odd how, amid all the carnage and chaos – the smashing of furniture, the screams, the shooting, the curses – there lay nothing between us but silence. A thick blanket of silence. Then he raised his chin and muttered, 'Let me die in the open air, man, nae under ma ain roof. Gimme that, at least.'

I had steeled myself against the usual pleas: *Let me live. Spare my wife. Pity the bairns*. This seemed such a small thing to ask, such a trivial mercy to grant: "Let me die in the open air."

I held his gaze and nodded. 'For your bread which I have eaten, I will.' We shoved him outside with our musket butts, and he stood there before us in his thin nightshirt, tartan plaid over one shoulder, his face underlit by the blood-spattered snow.

We raised our muskets.

He ripped off his plaid, threw it in our faces and ran. We ripped aside the flapping tartan and fired after him, but the night had already swallowed him up. Maybe he lived. Maybe he froze to death, being without his thick woollen plaid.

Part of me hopes he got clear.

But Campbell came down upon us in a spray of snow, frothing with rage as he wrenched around his horse's bridle. His sword was black with blood. 'There's two more run into the forest yonder!' he bellowed at me. 'Get after them and finish them both!'

I waded through the thick drifts into the forest, almost sinking up to my knees as my panting clouded the air. Before long I could hear them crashing through the deadwood; clods of snow slumped down from the branches, showing their panicked flight ahead clear as day. I followed their footprints through the trees – one set pressed deep, the other so small and light that it barely dented the snow. Pretty soon the snowy trees swallowed up the roar of burning buildings behind me, the distant crackle of muskets. All was silent when I finally found them: a silent grey hollow pillared with bare tree trunks. A woman and child clung gasping to each other, too exhausted to run any further, breath curling into the frosty air like musket smoke.

Good soldiers follow orders . . .
Good soldiers follow orders . . .
Good soldiers follow orders . . .

I raised my musket. Fired. Drew my pistol. Fired again.

And breathed out.

Twigs and snow tumbled down upon me from where the balls had holed the leafy canopy overhead. The woman stared at me, her hand clamped over the boy's mouth to stop him screaming.

Neither of us said a word.

Then I pulled the shawl from around her shoulders, turned on my heel and headed back, trudging through the snow. On the way, Providence set a wolf in my path, so I killed it and daubed the shawl with its blood. I'd have something to show Campbell. Appease his butcher's heart. Maybe.

Still, I'm glad they got away.

When I emerged from the frozen trees it was all over. Redcoats crowded the open ground before the smoking heaps of charred timbers. Fallen bodies littered the blood-spattered snow, strewn about like windblown leaves.

A charnel house. We were no longer men, proud and honourable. We were godless beasts.

A pitiful row of women was arrayed kneeling before the blackened ruins, hands bound tightly behind their backs. I could smell the bloodlust on the surrounding officers who panted like starving dogs, their eyes glazed and inhuman. A merciless ring of steel. The youngest of the shivering captives, no older than fourteen, began to sob. The tears poured hopelessly, down her cheeks, glistening like silver frost.

Campbell prowled behind the line like a restless wolf stalking prey, his flinty grey eyes stiff with contempt. He glanced my way. 'Finished 'em both off, did you?'

I held up the bloodstained shawl. 'Yes, sir,' I lied. 'They're both taken care of.'

'Good man.' He suddenly turned and drew his pistol in one fluid movement. Pressed it against the nearest prisoner's head.

And pulled the trigger.

The crack echoed over the devastated village. The woman crumpled to her knees, then pitched forwards onto her face. Blood seeped outward from her twitching corpse in a widening black stain. The other prisoners cringed into the snow, whimpering and moaning. A young private reeled away and vomited.

Campbell holstered his pistol. Nodded to his awaiting officers. 'Kill the rest of these bitches, then burn the bodies. We've delayed long enough. Save your lead.'

And the swords came out.

I'll never forget that night, for as long as I live.

It was a shameful night's work. I don't tell people I was there, in that valley of grim slaughter. I don't say, "I was at Glencoe." It's not some proud deed you brag of. You only have to mention the word and brawny clansmen shudder like frightened bairns. I shudder too: as if the snow blew deep inside me that night and lodged inside my heart, where it's never going to thaw.

And at five in the morning, I lie awake in the dark.

Shivering.

MUDLARK

It's a dreary grey evening in February, when Jonny Moreau gets caught again.

East along the great winding highway of the River Thames, thronged with slow chugging barges and coal launches belching black smoke, way down past Teddington and Richmond to Chiswick, and further downriver still: past Chelsea, the pleasure gardens spread bright with fountains and banners by day, with tree lamps and fireworks by night; past the domed spires of Whitehall where ministers drone through their weekly councils of state; past Holborn where the clerks of Lincoln's Inn hunch over ledgers and sigh up at the clock; past the Tower's chilly battlements guarded by croaking ravens and surly yeoman warders in scarlet and gold livery; past the tanneries and knackeries of Rotherhithe seeping their leathery stench into the river; past Ferris Ironworks pouring its endless drizzle of molten lead into vats and channeled moulds; further down still to where the Thames, wide and filthy-brown with the warm sour stink of sewage, swings in a great curve southwards . . .

This is Limehouse, and Jonny Moreau is getting a bollocking from his mother. Again.

His mum thinks he's nine years old, but she has a fuzzy memory rotted by drink; he might be eight, or seven, or maybe ten. His surname is French, but like his age that's a vague guess on his mum's part, because he looks more like a ragged guttersnipe from the St Giles rookery or a slab-faced runt from the Scottish Highlands, yet there's Irish and Nordic blood in him too and even a distant trace of Lascar from his mum's side. Jonny's not very bright, really, but he has that endearing clumsy tenderness that sometimes prompts him to hug his mum close and plant a sticky kiss on her ruddy cheeks. The poor woman's usually too addled by her penny-quart of gin to hug him herself; but she responds

151

warmly enough, once she realises.

Right now she's lolling in an armchair, ranting at him for filching a kidney pie. Feeble sunlight seeps in through cracked windowpanes and soot from the smoking fireplace veils the peeling wallpaper. Jonny stares at his tattered toeless shoes, only half listening to his mum's scolding. A brown streak of sopping gravy down his shirt proclaims his guilt.

Not his fault he was hungry. Not his fault he won't be fed at home, his belly growling from its meagre meal of watery gruel. He has a dull shilling in his pocket from a dockyard navvy for delivering a letter to his sweetheart, but he won't be wasting that on food, not pathetic table-scraps, not when there's easy pickings available for nothing. Not when you can snatch up so much at the Cable Street market for free if you've got a quick hand and a steady eye. Sometimes he strikes lucky and brings home a treasured morsel for his mum; a bruised apple or an orange or a half-gnawed lukewarm sausage roll. And she'll tut and wag a stern crooked finger under his nose and grumble, though they both know she's only joking. 'Yer a no-good thievin' rotter,' she'll smirk as she tickles him, until he's wriggling and squealing in her arms. 'If I 'ad me way, Jonny boy, yew'd be slavin' in the work'ouse.'

That was a damn good pie, he daydreams, remembering the hot gravy dripping over his fingers, toes curled in bliss on the steps of St Margaret's as he'd munched his steaming prize, meat and flaky pastry settling deep in his belly like glowing coals –

'Yew listenin' ta me, boy?'

Bony fingers clamp his chin and jerk his face around, into his mum's stern scowl. 'If yer pa were 'ere, 'e'd give yew what for,' she slurs around another mouthful of gin. 'Don't waste yer life, boy, thash what 'e'd say.' She glances aside at the battered fiddle propped against the mildewed wall. 'William Moreau, eh? French sailor, 'e were.' She's squinting at him now, blinking through her gin haze as she croons over fond memories. 'Real 'andsome. Yer pa played the fiddle so well, with such a fine voice. Dark hair. Nearly black. Like yours. And he weren't no stinking thief. *Ever*.'

Her eyes are glazed, tongue loosened by the dregs of gin. She slumps back into her armchair with a drunken giggle. Jonny winces; come nightfall she'll waddle downstairs and over to the dram shop in Rum Alley for another precious bottle.

Plenty of money pouring in to sate her thirst. With the boats moored up at the wharf and the workers at the nearby dockyards, she makes over five pounds on a good day. Sailors swagger through the slum streets and upstairs on wobbly sea-legs to thump on her door, eager for their evening grunt. No soft featherbed for them; a rag-strewn mattress for sixpence a go works just fine. The tattered red lampshades, the sickly-sweet stench of wilting roses on the windowsill. 'Looks real fancy,' Ma will giggle, shooing her son out the door and pulling the next customer inside.

Jonny knows when he's unwelcome. He runs away towards the river. Alone.

They corner him in the shadow of the tidal wall, thumping and kicking until he's groaning in the mud. A straw-haired lad shoves his way through the leering gaggle of boys, face twisted in scorn as he rips away Ma's silver ring. 'Look 'ere, mates. We all knows about Jonny Moreau, don't we? His ma's a seedy old tart –'

A shrill screech of rage. Someone rushes past Jonny, there's a sickening crack and the boys scatter like roaches. The blond runt scurries up the beach, cradling his mashed face and wailing like a scalded cat.

Jonny gapes in amazement. A young girl with fiery red curls scowls after them, a dark smear of bank mud across her cheek like proud warpaint. She helps him up. 'You okay?'

'Who're you?'

She beams at him, a flash of crooked yellow teeth. 'Name's Peggy.' By now the boys have all vanished. They've taken his ring, too.

Peggy wraps a comforting arm around him. 'Just ignore 'em,' she soothes, her fingers dancing over his ribs until he's squirming and giggling for mercy. 'They're nasty little shits, and nasty little shits ain't worth cryin' over.'

'Really?'

'Nah, course not.' She grabs his hand and pulls him up the shingle beach. 'C'mon! Let's go treasure hunting!'

It's Peggy who soon spies the blond ringleader lurking behind the fishmonger's, admiring his new plunder. It's Peggy who steals a net from the Costa family who do crabbing in Southwark.

Their winter nets are thick and heavy. Perfect for catching prey.

A glorious raid. The pair of them swoop down upon the gang, crowing in triumph and pelting them with lumps of soggy mud, until everyone soon resembles a pack of shrieking golems. Peggy helps ensnare the blond runt, thumping him until he whines for mercy. She pulls the ring free with a victorious whoop while Jonny sits on him and pulls his ears.

It's Peggy who shows him how to scale the crumbling wall at St Mary's graveyard; Peggy who shelters underneath the black barnacle-encrusted ribs of an upturned rowboat with her new brother-in-crime. Peggy clasps his hand in a fistful of mud and chants her solstice spells wishing summer will never end, then steals a sweet kiss over a half-empty bottle of cider with only pale white crabs to witness. He's king of Poplar that glorious week, clambering over slimy rooftops alongside Peggy, hooting like owls outside taverns. A comradeship she doesn't extend to any other boys in their small ragged band of thieves. Word spreads fast: half the urchin boys are terrified of her. *It's Peggy Jones,* they whisper, *watch out. She'll beat any boy in a running race, ties oyster knots tighter than yer grandpa ever could.* For days after, the blond runt crosses the street to avoid them, eyes averted, flinching like a whipped bitch.

Mudlarks they call themselves; first scornful labels of shame from sneering watermen, it soon becomes a badge of fierce pride. Their entire existence is spent squelching through the sucking mud, scooping up scraps of rubbish which might yield any glittering trinket of value, their eyes perpetually cast downward to the muddy tide as it spews its filthy treasures at their bare feet. An old copper brooch, green with age. A gleaming Roman coin. Chunks of sodden coal. A wicked railing spike, like an iron fang. Their muddy clothes are a jumbled mishmash of ragged garments cobbled together in grey, green and brown, sometimes threadbare coats stolen from corpses stumbled over upon the foreshore. At first a bright one will think up the plan, then ten more follow along like slippery silver eels through inky black water, scrambling over the moored barges shrieking like magpies.

Huge docks are clawing their way out of the sodden marshland of Rotherhithe and Wapping, bringing fresh new opportunities. So many boxes of fragrant tea and bales of cotton from the East Indies. Casks of brandy and crates of tobacco from North America. Bulging sacks of bitter-smelling coffee, barrels of rum and hogsheads of brown sparkling sugar from the West Indies. Iron, linen and tallow from the frozen Baltic states. Irish beef. Welsh coal. New Zealand wool.

With such a vast quantity, how could a little be missed?

Mudlarks are always light-fingered. The smaller boys would squeeze through broken boards into the gloomy warehouses then pass out whatever they could carry.

'What a shame, the cask is broke,' giggles one.

'Waste's an abomination, says the Lord,' another boy adds, straight-faced as a parson.

Soon they're stealing contraband to order which Peggy jots down in a tattered ink-stained notebook, scribbling the thefts of their scurrying raids along the riverside wharves. Most people pay to be rowed across the sluggish brown Thames, but other bribes work far easier; a handful of olives or a strip of salt beef always wins favour with the wherrymen, steering their nimble rowboats between the lumbering goods barges that clog the teeming waterway. A growing reputation would have to be maintained; Jonny feels himself pulled along the riptide of their criminality but soon the wave has already closed over his head before he realised.

Sometimes they'll pass the Execution Dock at Wapping, where newly-hanged smugglers and pirates swing in the breeze as a feast for crows and gulls. Jonny stares in fascination at the bloated corpses hanging from the riverside gibbet there, washed over by three high tides before they're finally cut down and buried in common unmarked holes. He's never been to a hanging before. Most Londoners have been part of that fickle baying mob watching the criminals' grisly punishment. Men, women and children flock around the gallows to jeer or boo each man dangling from the noose, throwing peelings and gnawed bones as they gasp out their last gargling breaths, feet kicking the air and heads twitching like hooked fish.

Peggy always averts her eyes from the swaying corpses. 'They keep the rope short at Wapping,' she mutters. 'So a man's neck don't snap, he chokes real slow . . .'

Before long she takes him to her home on Herring Street, where her drunken father and silent, defeated mother barely notice another small, dirty child in their midst. A warm house with a room upstairs, a fire of coals ready for winter, glass in the windows and always a spare loaf of bread in the cupboard. A generous slab of bread spread thickly with beef dripping. Best thing Jonny's ever tasted. Like him, Peggy is a law unto herself, living a wild gutter-rat life stealing from the bustling street markets.

Peggy's father is a failed ship chandler – originally his job had been to furnish ships with supplies for long journeys. But he's drunk the business slowly and surely away through rum and brandy, letting his sailcloth moulder and his fishing lines tangle. Besides, there are always ten other men with cheaper prices waiting to take his place. He is a man of tall stories and wild tales when deep into his dregs, stories peppered with foul language and bawdy laughter. Yet his jovial bonhomie soon drains away with the last dregs of liquor, and he sinks deeper into the refuge of his nightly bottle, sinking deeper into self-loathing. He's already barred from the Red Ox and White Lion for putting the wind up his fellow drinkers.

Jonny gazes across the table at the morose figure hunched by the smouldering fireplace and shudders. *Please, God*, he offers up a silent prayer, *don't let me end up like that. Ever.*

There's something very wrong when you arrive home at dusk, at a rundown stinking flat you know is occupied, but no one answers your call.

'Ma?'

He creeps upstairs, neck prickled.

'Ma, you there?'

No drunken singsonging from above. No laboured grunting, no creaking furniture, no faint moans of passion. Not even his mother's raspy snores that keep him awake well after midnight.

He peers into the dingy room, and his heart freezes.

His mother is sprawled in her armchair, arms hanging limp. Yellowed skin stretched over jutting cheekbones, the sheen of sweat glistening on her forehead.

'Ma!' He hurries over to kneel at her side.

'Hello, love,' she croaks, and reaches out. Jonny squeezes her trembling hand, strokes her slender fingers. He rests his forehead against her burning brow, her skin dry and hot to the touch. The deep hollows beneath her eyes are an ominous grey-blue.

161

'Oh, Ma,' he sighs, tears pricking his eyelids. She draws a laboured breath.

'I'm so sorry, Jonny,' she rasps, 'I –' She dissolves into a fit of coughing, wracked with tremors. Jonny rubs her back until the spasms pass.

'I'm sorry, love,' she whispers, 'I've been an awful mum.' She gropes for his hand. Jonny grasps it, fresh tears spilling down his cheeks at her feeble grip. She has always been his strength. His bulwark against the night, keeping the wolf from the door.

She fumbles with the silver flower ring on her left hand, tugs it free. Presses it into his palm. 'Promise me you'll keep this safe, my boy.'

'Please, Ma, don't tire yourself out.' His throat aches, the words barely forced out.

Her grip tightens. 'Promise me!'

He sniffles, scrubbing away tears with his free hand. 'That don't matter now. Just rest. We'll get you all better –'

'No!' Even though her voice is a reedy whisper, the fierceness makes Jonny's breath catch in his throat. 'You've worked so hard.' She holds his gaze even as her strength fades with every heartbeat. 'Don't ever give up, you hear me?'

He chokes. 'I . . . I won't.'

Her grip relaxes, her death mask cracks into a warm tender smile. Sunlight seems to flood the room, and his mother is back with him. 'My brave boy. I'm so proud of you, Jonny.'

Then her eyes flutter closed, her mouth clenches tight, and she begins to shake. Jonny grips her by her trembling shoulders, clings to her clenched fist to keep her still, keep her steady.

There is nothing more he can do.

His mother's body is in a place of hellish torture. It twists, it writhes, it buckles and strains, shivering like a windblown leaf. He can stay beside her, comfort her as best he can, but this fever is far too great, too viciously strong. An enemy too powerful for him. It has curled its tendrils about his mother and tightened its stranglehold, sank its claws deep, and is refusing to surrender her. It seeps a musky, dank, salty stink. Somewhere from far away, from a dark nightmare place of rot and wet. It gorges itself on pain and grief and torment. It is an insatiable, unstoppable evil; the worst, foulest kind of darkness.

Jonny does not leave her side. He cannot. He swabs her burning brow with the damp cloth, clasps her trembling hand, kisses her cheek whispering, 'Please, Ma, please don't leave me, please don't go.' None of it has pulled her back; none of it has saved her. He dampens the cloth again, wipes her sweaty forehead, strokes her hair. Feels his hope slowly begin to drain away, like water leaking from a punctured bucket. He is a fool, a blind idiot, the worst kind of simpleton for ever thinking he could save her.

She's convulsing now, flushed and panting, her stick-thin arms beating against the chair, her glassy gaze rooted upon the ceiling. Her heels drum relentlessly on the floor; a thumping, a hammering like onrushing thunder. Her cracked lips leak a hoarse keening whistle; her teeth rattle with every shudder. Anyone who has ever described dying as 'peaceful' or 'slipping away' has lied, has never witnessed it happen. Death is a violent struggle. The body fiercely clings to life as ivy to a wall, and will not easily surrender, will not willingly loosen its grip without a fight.

All at once she stops shaking, and a great hush fills the room. A soundlessness. A numbness. Her body falls still, motionless, her gaunt unseeing eyes fixed upward.

Her hand slackens in his.

And there, by a dead fire, held in the arms of her weeping son, in the dingy room in which she fed him, nursed him, smacked him and cuddled him, Ma draws her last rattling breath. A ragged, tired sigh.

In.

Out.

And then silence. Stillness.

Nothing more.

He learns that it *is* possible to cry all through the night. That there are so many different ways to cry: the sudden outpouring of fierce tears; the deep, racking sobs; the soundless and endless leaking of sorrow from his eyes, from every grieving pore.

Her cheeks are stretched thin, hollowed by fever. Her eyelids are a delicate greyish purple, like early spring petals. He closed them himself. With his own hands, his own trembling fingers, and how hot and slippery they had felt, how unmanageable that awful task, how difficult it had been to place his fingers over those lids, so dear, so familiar, and close them forever. How is anyone ever to shut the eyes of their own dead mother? The woman who bore him, raised him, scolded him, loved him? How is it possible to find two bitter-odoured pennies, worn smooth as river pebbles, and rest them there, heavy in the eye sockets, to weigh down those clammy lids? How can anyone bear to do this? It isn't right. It cannot be.

He jerks awake at midnight gasping for air. That murky brown torrent flooding through his nightmares. Sometimes it was Ma sinking into the crushing darkness far below him; other times it was Peggy. Once it was himself wading out into the churning current, pockets crammed with pebbles as Peggy watched from the riverbank and did nothing. Letting himself sink willingly into the silty blackness. Feeling a flash of blissful, joyous relief before he remembered the searing cold, the roaring dark.

The river took his mother. It'll take him too, in the end. It takes everything.

He cannot bear the morning. At dawn, parish men come and lift her into a narrow coffin of bare pine boards. They bind up her jaw with linen, swaddle her in cloth with a sprig of rosemary clasped in limp hands; she looks like the dead, pale, stern and fearless. She looks flatter and deader than corpses he has seen sprawled on the Thames foreshore, with their guts spilled out and crabs scuttling over their faces. He remembers that fateful night, only yesterday: her thrashing limbs, her forehead damp with sweat. Ma, he thinks, didn't you fight? If I had seen your death coming, if he had dared peer around the doorway, I would have thrown him down and smashed his skull to splinters on the floorboards; I would have crucified him against the wall, taken my knife and ripped him open from balls to brains.

He looks down at his mother and suddenly sees it, feels it, scents it. She is covered in the touches of other men. Drunken men. Clumsy men. Brutish men. Their grubby hands. Their filthy pawing gropes. All over her body, all over her skin, her hair, her pallid face, her pale hands, as if an animal has run across her over and over again, leaving tiny greasy pawprints.

He feels sickened. She is no longer his. She never was. She was theirs. Even in death, they took her from him too.

The parish men close the lid. His mother's face vanishes from sight. He leaves the room when they bring out the hammer and nails.

The long funeral march to the churchyard is worse. He walks behind the coffin, alone. The neighbours, the townsfolk in the street step aside when they see the silent procession. They put down their tools, their baskets. They edge backwards onto the pavements, clearing the way. Men remove their hats, cross themselves. Mothers clutch their children a little closer. They call out words of comfort, of sorrow. They send up prayers – for the mother, for the orphaned boy, for themselves. Some of them weep.

A hansom cab slows to a halt ahead. The driver doffs his hat. 'God rest her soul!' he calls. From the dim gloom of his carriage, pale moustached faces peer out, eyes creased in pity beneath their top hats.

He cannot bear the sympathetic gaze of the mourners, cannot meet their eyes as his mother is slowly lowered into the sour wet soil of St Mary Magdalene churchyard. He lets their meaningless murmurings wash over and around him. He doesn't want their sympathy and their prayers and their soft words of gentle comfort. He hates the way onlookers stood aside to let the coffin pass and then regrouped behind them, erasing their passage as if it were nothing, as if it never were. He wants to take his iron spike and gouge deep into the ground, to hack into the cobbled street beneath him so there will forever be a mark, so it will always be known hereafter that Ma came this way. *She was here. She was real. She was my mum.*

'God had need of her,' the parson murmurs to him after the service, laying a wizened hand on his shoulder.

Jonny wrenches free and turns on the man, almost snarling, filled with the vicious urge to strike him down, to sink his fist deep into that frowning face and relish the splintering crunch of bone beneath his knuckles. *I* needed her, he wants to scream, and your God should have waited His turn. He wants to bare his teeth and roar. Rage at the unfairness. Tear this cruel uncaring world asunder, for what it robbed him. His mother cold and decaying beneath the churchyard sod.

Instead he says nothing. He clenches his fists and stomps away, the bitter taste of injustice heavy on his tongue like coffee sludge. He wanders aimlessly through the marketplace, past the fortuneteller stall and the organ grinder and the fruit seller, under the sickly yellow haze of the gas lamps. Distant bloodthirsty roars of spectators echo from a rat-baiting pit, mixed with snarling dogs and the shrill death-squeals of trapped vermin . . . Jonny sags against the damp brick wall, his head throbbing. Somewhere a bottle tinkles over cobblestones. A cat yowls.

There will be no going back from this. No undoing of what has passed. His mother has gone and he is alone and his shrivelled belly will always cry out for food and the gulls will still circle above the Thames every day. Time flows only one way.

On the gateposts of Christ Church are two snarling stone lions that his mother had once lifted him up to look at, but he had squirmed away crying in fear. They sit there still, twin haughty glares on their faces. With a sudden surge of rage he scoops up a handful of mud and hurls it at the nearest one, a thick black gobbet of muck splattering over that smug snarling snout. *Wipe that smirk off your face*, he thinks.

The next day brings more scavengers. Like all shrewd folk mired in grinding poverty, Ma had laid cash aside. She had lived thriftily, her only extravagance the nightly gin bottle, money squirrelled safely away. But as soon as she's deep in the cold uncaring earth, it all falls apart with amazing speed, her savings devoured. First the landlord's man arrives for his due payment. Their house had never been owned, only leased. The rent is in arrears, and all the furniture has to be sold to pay for it. The bailiffs come for their pound of flesh, just like the hungry sailors. They swarm into the dingy lodging house, tramp upstairs and strip Ma's attic room to its bare bones. Like ravenous gulls leaving a corpse picked clean of meat.

Jonny watches numbly as the bailiffs carry everything outside. Every cup, every bent spoon, the tattered red lampshades . . . even the armchair Ma had died in, scarcely cold, is hoisted up and carted away. Only a dank musty tenement room under a sloped ceiling of rotting rafters, the rank stench of boiled cabbage seeping through the flimsy walls and mouse shit mushed into the floorboards. But it was theirs. Their fortress against want. Their meagre precious kingdom for six shillings and ninepence a week. It was *home*.

And now it isn't. An empty, cheerless void.

The wilted roses lie trampled in a puddle,

silently drowning.

Jonny can't bear to watch any longer. He runs away towards the river. Alone.

Abandoned to fend for himself, Jonny slowly sinks deeper into the cloying familiar comfort of London's mud. That claggy, foetid layer of clay that smothers all of London, clinging to boot soles and carriage wheels, but most of all gathers on the Thames foreshore, across those wide, stinking festering mudflats that crawl down to the open sea.

Elsewhere the thick London clay is put to use, squashed and baked into bricks to fuel the building of this ever-growing ravenous city, but on the Thames riverbanks it only traps things. Chunks of driftwood. Metal. Bones. Pottery shards, some centuries old. All are swallowed and churned in the thick rotting mulch. It claims the bodies of the murdered and the suicides off Blackfriars Bridge, whose watery graves that great silver snake, the Thames, vomits out along with animal carcasses before sucking them down into the foul slime. Jonny picks through this sludgy detritus with other ragamuffin children who squabble over the river's offerings.

A stable on Primrose Lane is their meagre refuge from rain and wind, huddled together for warmth like mice in a nest. Shivering in their threadbare clothes, they're gently lulled to sleep by the sweet smell of hay and the warm musty breath of dozing horses. If he's lucky and quick, Jonny gets to wash at the water trough before anyone else catches him. But he rarely gets the chance, though. Soon the mudlarks all stink to high heavens with a thick tideline of grime smeared on their necks, wrists and ankles.

One blustery grey day, a bald parson in solemn black picks his way gingerly down to the foreshore to preach to the ragged band of vagabonds. He wrinkles his nose at the children's stench, holds a perfumed handkerchief over his mouth.

'Where do you live, child?' he asks. Jonny's hungry eyes are fixed on the hard wheat loaf in the man's hand.

'London, sir.'

'And where *is* London, young man?'

Jonny can smell the bread. Maybe this stupid man was lost?

'London's in England, sir. And England is in London,' he adds quickly. For these forgotten

173

ragtag children, London is the only world they would ever know.

The man's lip curls. 'Have you heard of Jesus Christ, child?'

Jonny shrugs. 'Heard of him, p'raps. Dunno who he is, though, and I don't much care.' His eyes flicker back to the bread and eventually the preacher hands it over, shaking his head sadly.

'Are you a God-fearing child, boy?'

Jonny bristles. God-hating, more like. God didn't spare the life of his mother. The highest things in his watery world are the church steeples. Nowhere to run in all these mean twisted streets, even out onto this muddy foreshore, where some watchful steeple does` not loom. As soon as one of them is hidden by the crooked elbow of a lane, there's always another staring sternly down from behind the chimneys. And under every steeple: the House of God. A dazzling vault of light inside, so much open space it could terrify a boy from Tanner's Lane. Merciless sunlight blasting down from huge arched windows, with no kindly shadows anywhere. No charity in its cold grey stones.

But he still feels a warm flush of pride every time he passes by the Christ Church gates;

despite his gnawing sadness and the gaping emptiness of his life, all the rain in the world hasn't yet managed to wash the mud out from that lion's nostrils.

He sits crosslegged on the shingle beach, gazing listlessly out across the churning brown river. Ma is gone. His home is gone. There's nothing left for him here. Just the ragged clothes on his back and a single silver ring, its petals uncurling towards the feeble sun. From now on, a bleak grey future grubbing out his miserable wretched existence amongst the riverbank's clinging filth, crawling through the mud for scraps.

A shadow falls across him. 'Been looking for you.' He doesn't react as Peggy sits down beside him, frowning. 'You all right?'

He scoops up a fistful of grit and hurls it into the water with a hiss. 'Course not.'

Her gaze softens. 'Sorry about your ma. She were real nice.'

Jonny swallows down a fresh wave of bubbling grief. Blinks away his tears. 'Thanks. But . . . I got nothin' left. No family. No home.'

Peggy slips her grubby hand into his and squeezes gently. 'You've still got *me*, remember.'

Then she blushes, rummages in a pocket. 'Found this yesterday. Saved it for you.'

She pulls out a plain bronze signet ring and gently slips it onto his forefinger. Simple and unadorned by stone or inscription, it fits him perfectly. Jonny swallows down the sudden lump in his throat. 'Thanks. It . . . it's beautiful.' He takes Peggy's hand and slides Ma's ring onto her finger.

Peggy rests her head on his shoulder, holding out her hand and cooing with delight as the silver flower glints in the sunlight. 'See? Matching set. We're partners now. I ain't goin' nowhere.'

Warmth blooms deep in his chest. He presses a fond kiss to Peggy's cheek as her thumb strokes over his knuckles. Her hand curled tight in his, Ma's ring gleaming on her hand alongside his signet ring.

He still dreams of the river, that relentless thundering torrent. He's no longer drowning. No one is. Though they will all sink down into the crushing dark one day. Him. Peggy. His mother's precious ring, buried deep in rotting darkness. And the last few minutes may be horrible, but that's okay. Because nothing's ever truly lost. The Thames will keep on flowing and there will be blossom in springtime and the gulls will still soar above the river.

Time only flows one way. For even after the darkest, cruellest winters, there's always the spring. And there always will be.

They run away along the riverbank.

Together.

BROTHERHOOD

It's not a gunshot that jerks Luke awake. It's the moans.

Then he hears the dull patter of rain against the window and thinks: *Again? Fuck.*

That low, unending keening that echoes through the walls and sets his teeth on edge. Punctured with jagged gasps, the agonised whimper of an animal trapped behind bars, like Sam's trying so hard to bite down on his screams and stop them spilling out from clenched teeth.

Doesn't work.

It could be the growl of thunder melting into the booming roar of howitzers, or the pounding rain that echoes the death-crackle of rifle fire, or the howling of the wind dissolving into the screams of dying men – it doesn't matter, really. Luke knows the nightmares always come crawling in the dark; shrieking ghosts dripping red with clawed hands and pale burning eyes. Walls splashed with the blood of his friends. He's spent many a long night whimpering into the darkness, whenever the storms sweep overhead.

The first time, it's the short choked-off cry that rips him from his fever dreams. Leaves him staring at the ceiling on the wrong side of midnight, watching the cockroaches scuttle across the flaky walls.

Ten minutes later, it's the footsteps. Sam paces his bedroom next door, making the floorboards groan. He passes by Luke's door, softly muttering to himself in the stairwell. But no matter how quiet Sam might think he is, his brother can still hear him.

Then barely an hour later, just when Luke's eyelids begin to droop: the moaning. He waits. Finally, a soft, hesitant tap on his door.

Because Sam . . . Sam doesn't ask for help. Ever. But his face is chalk-white, every corner etched deep with tension, hands trembling, and the request couldn't be more blatant if he'd screamed it aloud. His eyes are wet and haunted, face sunken and tired in the way Luke remembers being tired. Hollowed out, like a gnarled tree stricken with rot. The ghosts of long miserable nights hunched beside guttering fires in the pouring rain, ice shivering through your bones and mud seeping into your socks, nothing but gruel churning in your hollow belly. Acrid smoke choking the lungs, the stink of charred flesh, writhing shadows howling like demons under a choking green sea. Or braced shoulder-to-shoulder in the broken earth while the enemy guns sweep away the friends beside you, butchers' meat splashed to the four winds, and afterward an ash-grey sky full of diving crows.

Blood. Mud. Stabbing beaks. Hooked talons. Ripping. Tearing. Luke blinks away the memories.

'Bed too soft?' he asks. Sam flinches.

'Sorry,' he shrugs, carefully avoiding Luke's eyes. 'S'all right, just . . . damn pillow keeps me up nights. Like I'm sinkin' right through the floor.' A brief flickering smile. It's bright and jarring and fools Luke for exactly zero seconds. Because he *knows* that pleading look in Sam's bleak eyes, that crack in his brother's mask that just screams 'Please don't leave me.'

'Hey, c'mon,' he beckons, and leads Sam downstairs. Sam follows, fists clenched. Max meets them at the front door with a joyful bark, tail thumping with eagerness. Luke passes his brother a stout blackthorn stick. The darkness outside is streaked silver with rain.

Sam blinks. 'What're you . . . ?'

Luke just nods at the open door. 'Go on. Trust me. Take your time. No rush.' His brother hesitates, then grunts and trudges out into the drizzle, Max dancing around his legs.

Luke watches them fade into the rain. Beth joins him, leaning against the doorjamb and gazing sadly after her husband. 'Bad dreams again?' she sighs, rubbing Luke's back.

'We'll be okay.' Luke watches until they disappear into the blackness, then slips upstairs to the kitchen.

He heats milk whisked with nutmeg and honey, sweet and warm. Then bubble and squeak with greens, fried in butter. The potatoes sizzle and hiss in the skillet, crispy and gold. The carrots look very small and tender. Tiny pearl onions. Sam always liked small veg. A rich earthy smell. For Sam, the brother who reached out first. For Sam, the sergeant who led his men through the choking fires of war, and still brought them safely home.

The rain drums against the window. Five minutes. Ten.

The door creaks downstairs. A frantic pattering of claws before Max skitters into the room and snuffles around Luke, tail thrumming against his legs. A minute later Sam shuffles in, trailing the cold like a shroud, his face pale and jaw clenched.

But his hands aren't shaking anymore.

'Sit there,' Luke orders. Sam slumps into the armchair, staring fixedly at the floor. Max curls around his ankles, looking thoroughly pleased. His fur is matted with mud. He stinks of the river.

Thump. Thump. Thump.

Luke brings over the steaming mug of cocoa, and Sam's eyes widen and widen like this is nothing he ever expected.

'What —' he tries, and Luke just shrugs. Sam doesn't rely on him. Never has. He shouldn't rely on him, that's okay. They're brothers; they've always leaned on one other. But Sam's body deserves soft things right now, Sam's body deserves comfort, *Sam* deserves comfort.

'It'll help,' he says, and hopes it's true. He brings the plate over, Max's eyes tracking his every move. So many gifts, and the way Sam never stops being surprised when he eats something good, something Luke cooked just for him. He hopes this feels like a gift for his brother, maybe, this patchwork mess of steaming leftovers, but he's not sure –

'Oh, *fuck*,' Sam groans, slumping back against the wall with his eyes closed. 'I always hated collards when I was a kid. Mum used to boil the hell out of 'em, d'you remember?' He chuckles wetly. 'We ate 'em like four times a week, and I *hated* 'em.'

'I can make something else,' Luke offers, but Sam just smiles and pulls his plate closer.

'Don't you *dare*,' he mutters, and sniffles as he eats, but he's grinning through his tears. And afterwards, Max curled up against his chest, Luke hears Sam quietly weeping in Beth's arms as she murmurs soothingly to him.

'I miss her,' he hears, soft and cracked through the bedroom wall, 'I miss Mum, so damn *much*,' and Luke thinks*, god, Mum, do I miss you too.*

'Nnngh . . . Christ save me, I'm done for.'

'For shit's sake, Sam. Quit whingeing.'

Sergeant Sam Ward slumps against the broken brick wall, sweating and groaning like the melodramatic little shit he is. Trust his luck to be the only one seriously injured after that vicious hand-to-hand scuffle with German *Stoßtruppen*. 'Jesus, Mary 'n' Joseph,' he moans, clutching his shoulder. 'I'm gunna *die*.'

A chorus of annoyed groans from the rest of his patrol, scattered around the half-crumbled house. Tim Riley rolls his eyes. 'It's only dislocated, Sam. Don't be such a bloody wimp.'

'Fuck you, Riley,' Sam snarls back. 'It's fallin' off, I can't feel me fingers. Lord save me . . . Auuugghhhh. Send me 'ome, Sarge, I'm done with this war.'

Sergeant Luke Ward grins and squats beside his brother, trying (and utterly failing) to look sympathetic. 'Sorry, Sammy, you ain't gettin' out of it so easy,' he teases cheerily. 'C'mere, let's put it back. Quit bawlin', ya big baby.'

Lewis chuckles somewhere behind them, and doesn't even bother to offer any help. He's busy going through the grey-coated bodies with Rob, trying to find decent trophies to loot. Sam whimpers and shakes his head, shrinking away from Luke's outstretched hands and raising his good arm in defence. 'No no, don't touch it! You'll make it worse!'

Ed sniggers from the loft overhead. 'Get it together, Sammy – me liddle *sister's* got bigger bollocks than you!'

His mates chuckle as Luke slaps Sam's hand away, frowning mournfully at him. 'It ain't gunna fix itself,' he soothes. 'Trust me, Sam, I've done this a thousand times.' Well . . . maybe twice. He doesn't really know how painful it is, but it can't be that bad, right? It isn't even *bleeding*, for Christ's sake. 'It'll slide right back into place. You won't feel a thing – promise.'

Ed snorts so loud it's a wonder no German shells come crashing down upon them. 'Yeah, listen to 'im, Sarge knows what he's talkin' about.'

Luke grips Sam's shoulder tight. 'On three, Sammy.' Sam puffs and clenches his jaw. Braces himself.

'Ready?'

Sam meets his eyes and nods.

'One –'

CRACK.

Sam shrieks so loud that Luke nearly dislocates it again from shock. He cringes as his brother's cry echoes back at them from all corners of the desolate Belgian village. If there are any Hun sharpshooters lurking among the ruins, they're fucked for sure, but thankfully there's no answering battle cry or bullets whistling in. Luke lets him sag onto the damp straw floor, writhing around and swearing buckets. The sergeant's face is the epitome of cherubic innocence. 'What? I fixed it, didn't I?'

'Fuck you!' Sam wriggles over to snap furiously at his brother's ankles. 'Ya sneaky bastard – nngghh. Wanker!'

'Laaanguage,' Ed sing-songs above.

'Fuck off, shit'ead!'

The others tease him and leave him wheezing and cursing on the floor as Luke hurries to the doorway where rifleman Harry Carter stands guard. 'Tim, give Sam some of your holy water, won't you?'

Tim looks up from the small wooden horse he's carving. 'Holy water, sir?'

Luke rolls his eyes. 'The brandy you keep stashed in your second canteen. The one you think *I* don't know about.'

Tim blushes and hurries over to Sam. 'Yessir!'

Luke looks over to the lads huddled in the corner bickering over a game of Rummy, and suddenly his chest aches with a fierce surge of pride. They've come such a long way since he first roared at them in Basic Training, crawling through mud and bayoneting straw dummies. Now they're *his* boys, battle-hardened warriors, all of them fearless and indomitable in a firefight with a dozen battlefields christened with their blood: Jack Murray, the giant of a man still wearing that damn bowler hat instead of the standard-issue tinpot helmet, brow furrowed as he scribbles a letter for his Tyneside sweetheart; Paul Jones lounging in the straw halfway through his third smoke of the hour, eyes twinkling at some hidden joke as he cradles his Woodbines in fingerless mitts; Harry Carter, gaunt-cheeked and grimacing, sucks a toothpick as he notches fresh kills into his rifle butt with his bayonet; John Bryce spoons down Maconochie stew as if it's the finest peach ambrosia instead of beef gristle, mushy carrots and under-boiled turnip, with stubbled cheeks and that hideous hand-knitted scarf from his mother back in Newcastle. This isn't Basic, after all; on the front lines nobody gives a damn what you wear as long as you follow orders.

It's a welcome change, really – all of them sitting together and being civil, a tranquil respite from the long miserable nights huddled in flooded trenches in the endless drizzle, ice shivering through your bones and freezing mud seeping into your socks as the shells shriek down and the earth swallows screams. Or stacking sodden sandbags knee-deep in grimy mud to the endless dull boom of distant howitzers, cherished home letters clutched tight to their hearts like lifelines amid the creeping stench of mustard gas and the churning fear that gnaws the belly.

He'll miss this, when the war's over. They're blood brothers, Northmen in grimy khaki, one of a kind – despite all their petty squabbles over dice and cards, and the casual insults they sling his way.

A rat scuttles out of the gloom; it pauses amid the filthy floor and glares around, as if it's the lord of the manor and they're illegal squatters intruding on its turf.

'Hey, who's hungry?' Owen smirks, laying down a winning hand. The others boo and flick their cards at him.

Tim hauls Sam back onto his feet, patting his back in commiseration. 'I know, I know – it sucks,' he mutters, letting Sam swig from his canteen. 'Sergeant Ward couldn't keep a promise if you smeared it in glue and shoved it up his arse.'

'Careful, Tim – that's insubordination,' Paul sniggers.

'I was *drunk*,' Luke grumbles in mock-horror. 'I was *so* drunk when I offered all you layabouts the King's Shilling.'

'Nah – don't beat yerself up over it, Sarge,' Lewis chuckles, still rummaging through a corpse's pockets on the floor. 'We were all piss-drunk when we took it, too.'

Luke jerks awake with a muffled gasp, tearing out of a clawing blackness of whispering ghosts. Acid churning in his gut. Nausea hot and sour in his throat. His legs are tangled in sheets; he kicks them away as he heaves himself up, groping at his bedside for a revolver that isn't there. Panting, disorientated, he fights down a fresh wave of nausea and clenches his hand tight, curled up until his heart stops hammering and his breathing steadies. He lets himself slump back

189

down from the tensed half-rise he'd twisted himself into. Glances at the clock: ten past four. Only a few hours until dawn.

A mournful whine from the foot of his bed. He flinches as Max heaves himself up onto the bed with a disgruntled huff, nuzzling a cold wet nose into his hand. *Warm-rough-damp* rasps over his fingers.

'Wrong freakshow,' Luke mutters, as if an animal can understand a word he says, but Max just snorts, pads close and flops down, snuggled against Luke's chest. The room instantly smells of old dog.

Fine, he thinks, annoyed and grateful all at once. *Be that way*. He idly scratches Max's head, and the collie dog's tail thumps against his legs. Warm wiry fur under his fingers.

A door clicks shut downstairs. He rises up, unease crawling through him. The garden is bathed in moonlight. A black figure trudging across the lawn, towards the shelter of the trees. Makes sense. Sam needs some fresh air too.

Luke quietly slips out of bed and creeps downstairs. Warm and inviting as his bedroom is, it doesn't soothe him.

His family garden is as picturesque under

moonlight as it was in the afternoon sun. A cloudless night overhead, awash with glittering stars. The curving gravel paths are carefully kept, like the picturesque bushes and trees lining them, and one never has to look far for a beautiful place to sit. He'd spied a great spot earlier that day; a bench underneath an ancient oak with heavy branches that nearly kissed the ground. Through the foliage, shafts of moonlight dapple the lawn beneath. It exudes an air of peaceful seclusion in an already isolated village garden.

Then he sees the faint orange glow, shielded by a cupped palm; the faint plume of cigarette smoke rising like dawn mist from the hunched shadow. Somehow, he isn't surprised.

Sam looks around as his brother brushes aside the leaves. He raises a hand in greeting and shuffles over as Luke sits beside him, then waves a hand at the moonlit branches above.

'Nice place.'

'Mm,' Luke replies. Sam glances aside and smiles.

'You too, huh?'

His brother doesn't need to ask. 'Me too.'

Sam nods. 'Didn't feel right. I've never slept on a proper bed for so long.'

Luke grins. 'Too soft, right?'

'And not lumpy enough!'

They chuckle. After a comfortable silence, Sam glances up at the dark windows above. 'Hope Rosie and Mark are sleeping well.' He smiles at the image; both children curled up in their soft feather beds and gently snoring into their pillows. Maybe Rosie still has that doll safely clutched in her hands.

Luke hums in sympathy. He'd had the best sleep he could recall during these past two weeks. No neighbouring private stifling their sobs a few feet away. No distant wail of the Reveille bugle at dawn. No booming echo of howitzers to jolt you awake. He even slept the whole night through now; he called it sleeping in.

'Moved my blankets to the floor,' Sam mumbles. 'Still can't sleep without hearing the wind blowing outside. Thought I'd give it a try here, but it's still too quiet.'

Only the gentle rustling of leaves and a low buzz of insects broke the silence here. Nothing like the roaring of distant guns.

'And there ain't enough bodies jostling me around,' Luke adds. 'Y'know, I've never slept alone before. Never without someone an arm's reach from me.'

'Yeah, there were always blokes everywhere. What was your bed like?'

'An old greatcoat, real tatty. You?'

'Soggy sandbags. Duckboard for a pillow.'

'All through the war?'

'Long as I can remember.'

'Me too.'

Sam sighs. 'Sometimes . . .' He straightens up, shuffles beyond the screen of leaves and gazes up at the stars. 'Sometimes they'd take someone in the night. Always the weak ones who copped it. Or the cripples. You'd wake up and your neighbour was gone. Or worse . . . you'd see it happen. Boys screaming for their mums, carted off god-knows-where.'

Luke places a hand on his brother's shoulder. Sam hangs his head.

'The rats were awful,' he mumbles. 'You'd lie awake at night and hear them just outside. Rustling and squeaking . . . ugh.' He shudders. 'Or else you'd be chatting to a friend, sharing a smoke, and then' – he snaps his fingers – 'gone, just like that. Damn snipers.' He raises another cigarette with trembling fingers.

Luke waits.

'They don't know what they have,' Sam finally whispers. He raises an arm to encompass the slumbering neighbourhood, roof tiles silver in the moonlight. 'Peace and quiet. They think all this is normal. To sleep on a soft comfortable bed. To not unstick your boots from the mud every morning. To not wake up crawling with lice.'

Luke gives a wry chuckle at that. 'To be fair, you were never really keen on baths, were you?'

Sam swats him playfully. 'My point stands!' The silence stretches again, then he sighs. 'Martin wanted to hear all about the front.'

Luke gapes. 'What? Uncle Martin?'

Sam nods miserably. 'Wanted to know if I'd ever killed a Hun up close, with my bare hands – Christ, I wanted to smack him!' He mashes his cigarette into the soil, fuming. 'And then he said, "terrible business, with the gas and all the rest of it" . . . how could he even *say* that?!'

Luke shudders. Third Company all stiff and blue-faced in death, stretched against the parapet or sprawled in the dugouts, their faces frozen in ghastly screams . . .

Sam sniffles, wipes his nose on his sleeve.

'I . . . I miss the lads, now I'm home.'

Luke squeezes his shoulder. He couldn't help but fondly recall his mates at Ypres. Good old Captain Barry Griffin, wise and hardbitten, flayed down to flint by war yet still doling out jokes over breakfast, with a remarkable nose for dirty weather, good food, and soft jobs; Owen Gray, gaunt-cheeked and cheerful, already on his third cigarette of the morning as he scribbled a letter to his Exeter sweetheart; Harry Carter, who'd beaten him bloody one night for filching his cigarettes, who'd given Luke his first swig of rum before first watch, who'd taught him how to hunt rats in the mudhole they called a dugout. John Bryce, steadfast and kind, quietly sharing his meagre rations with the younger boys, tucking into his mess-tin of bully beef as if it was a fine Savoy three-course dinner instead of cold jellied spam. All of them sleeping in mud, slime and blood. A foxhole brotherhood to the end.

Luke thinks of the days yet to come, when they'd finally be able to call this village home. It's the most peaceful, serene place he'd ever known. But Sam is right; its inhabitants knew nothing of the horrors of war. All they had was the silent list of names on the village memorial.

Lest we forget . . . yet Luke knows the bitter truth. They would never truly understand.

Perhaps someday he could forgive them for it.

He glances aside, and ice crawls down his spine: Sam's hunched over in the corner of the bench, head down and shoulders slumped. It's a posture of abject misery that feels like a boot to the chest, and has Luke shuffling over fast.

'Shit, matey,' he says, squeezing Sam's knee. 'Hey, what's wrong?'

Sam shakes his head and then lifts it. He isn't crying like Luke expected, but he looks confused. Overwhelmed. Lost.

'Sorry, sorry,' he mumbles. 'I just . . .' He turns glassy eyes on Luke. 'D'you ever feel . . . as if there's too much building up inside you, like –' He shakes his head again, waves a helpless hand. 'I can't explain it.'

'Try,' Luke murmurs.

Sam blushes, stares at his boots. 'You'll just laugh at me.'

'I'll do that anyway.' Luke chuckles as Sam swats his arm. 'C'mon. Let's talk. You can get it off your chest. And *then* I'll laugh at you.'

'Bastard.'

'Hey, what are brothers for?'

Sam sighs. 'I feel like . . . like everything's dialled up to eleven,' he grits out. 'I was laying there thinking how lucky – how *happy* I was, and it grew bigger and bigger, and then it – I couldn't stop thinking about all the alternatives, what if things had happened any other way, how – stupidly small our chances were. And I thought if I kept being around you I . . . I'd burn up. Like Private Jones who got caught in that mortar and all that was left behind was his boots.'

'Has anyone ever told you you're a morbid little shit?' Luke asks, and Sam snorts. 'Has this happened before?'

'Yeah,' Sam mutters. 'It usually just goes away without making me –' He balls up a fist. Luke places his hand over it and feels his brother slowly unclench. 'Do something I didn't want to,' Sam finishes, staring glumly at the whispering trees. 'I thought this time would be different.'

'Stay put,' Luke says, 'for just a second, okay?' and scurries off to the kitchen, thinking quickly. He's certain he's figured it out by the time he returns with two glasses.

'Alcohol won't fix this,' Sam frowns, even as he's taking one.

'Bully for you, this is ginger ale,' Luke smirks, and Sam chuckles. 'Kettle's slow as molasses and I can't be arsed to bring out a beer, so. Next best thing.'

'Thanks, anyway,' Sam smiles. He taps their glasses together, the bright ring of crystal. 'Cheers.'

'It's not a cure for anything, y'know,' Luke says, once Sam's thrown back his glass like it's a shot of whiskey. 'Loving somebody. Being around them. It's not going to turn your world upside down and fix all your problems.' Sam's grimace betrays how he'd been hoping that, at least a little. 'But I can see how it's frustrating that it might make stuff *worse*.'

'It just – hurts,' Sam mumbles. 'Thinking, y'know . . . even when I'm happy, something's there, niggling at me, making me remember all the ways I could lose somebody.'

'That's life, buddy,' Luke shrugs, 'kicking you when you're down.'

Sam groans and slumps back; Luke swats his knee. 'Hey, hey. Stay with me. All the dead we saw, out there . . . I *know* how that can shut you down. And what, you thought you could just bottle it all up inside and sweat it out like a bloody martyr? Without telling us? I'm your *brother*, damn it. Beth's your *wife*.'

'Didn't want to be a bother,' Sam mumbles to his boots.

Luke sighs and takes his hand. 'It ain't something you can fix yourself. You get sucked down that rabbit hole, there's no telling how deep you'll fall. Or how you'll pull yourself out again. And if you shut us out, if you make yourself alone, that is the quietest, most personal hell.' He squeezes Sam's shoulder. 'You know what I think, though? It'll get better. Most things do, in one way or another.'

Sam's pout is adorable. 'You think I'm making a huge fuss out of nothing?'

Luke raises his open palms in mock surrender. 'I didn't say *that*. Maybe it's – maybe you've got to walk before you can run. Maybe you've got to practice being happy before you can go all the way up to the stars.'

'Goddamn demoralising,' Sam mutters.

'I dunno,' Luke shrugs. 'I think it's kind of beautiful. That you can be paralysed by joy. That it's overwhelming, sometimes. Being happy. Enjoying the little things. And anyhow, we'll be with you every step of the way.'

Sam gives him another of those startled owlish expressions, wide-eyed and unblinking, before he leans over and rests his head on Luke's shoulder. Luke puts down his glass and hooks an arm across Sam's back, like he's trying to keep his brother from floating away.

'Stop doing that,' Sam grumbles into his chest. 'Being so . . .' He flaps a hand.

'Sorry,' Luke grins. 'I'll work on being a shithead.' Sam huffs a laugh, and something uncurls deep in Luke's chest, warm and blooming. He glances aside, and blushes; Sam is beaming fondly at him. 'What's that look for, you dumb shmuck?'

'*You*,' Sam smiles. 'Here, in our garden. Was – was it everything you ever wanted? When you used to daydream about it? Coming home again?'

Yes, Luke realises with startled gladness. All the blessings he hadn't counted before. Flowers he couldn't name, then. Quaint rosy-brick cottages bathed in dawn sunlight. Honeysuckle drooping over the eves, lavender spilling out between fence rails, a riot of honeybees. Kindly neighbours. Laughing children playing in the long grass. Never being alone anymore. Sinking into soothing warmth as steam coils around him, his bones turning to rubber; even after everything else, there's always the clawfoot tub. A nice long hot bath . . .

'Yeah,' he mumbles, his throat feeling gritty and strange. 'Of course. It's better, even.'

'It's incredible,' Sam murmurs, voice hushed with awe. He gazes out into the dark, beyond the climbing roses. 'I – I'd imagined – I thought about it a lot. Us, being together. You, happy. Wherever we were.'

'I was,' Luke nods. 'I was. I *am*.' Sam lays his head on his shoulder again with a weary sigh.

'Don't tell Beth about all this,' Sam sniffles. 'Please. I don't want her to worry. That'd only make things worse.'

'You're brave,' Luke comforts him. 'You really are.' They sit together in the darkness, Luke idly rubbing his brother's back.

'You busy tomorrow?'

'Dunno,' Sam murmurs sleepily. 'Rosie's itching to get a new birdhouse fixed up but Brian's been badgering me to help weed his garden – odds are he'll mount a village-wide manhunt if I'm still AWOL by lunchtime. We'll figure something out.'

'Grumpy old codger at number six, right?' Luke asks, and Sam hums a yes. 'Invite him over, he can help me fix the wheelbarrow.'

A muffled snigger. 'He'll paint it all in green, just you watch –'

'As long as it *works*.'

'He'll probably try to sweet-talk you into tinkering with his auger.'

Luke shrugs, jostling Sam's head. 'Joke's on him. If it means I can fuck around with a veg plot next spring, maybe I'll *let* him.'

Crickets chirp in the bushes, the endless comforting buzz of night echoing all around them. Luke had read, somewhere, that little things like this are good healers for the brain – fish tanks, too. Logs crackling in a fireplace, golden sparks rising like dancing fireflies. Mesmerising patterns calming the eyes, relaxing frazzled senses, soothing tired nerves. He remembers those first long sleepless weeks home where every bat and badger going about its nightly business had startled him out of bed, shivering against the wall at every faint nighttime rustle; he'd fallen asleep on the hearthrug more than once. Or else curled up rigid under the blankets on the wrong side of midnight, ears perked for the faintest noise, flinching at every house-settling creak and every bug hitting the window. On the real bad nights, convinced that he deserved it, he'd tried to count all the men he'd ever killed, their pallid faces swimming before his eyes – a shallow penance he'd quit once he'd realized this self-absorbed wallowing wasn't helping anyone. He still aches about wanting to *do* something substantial, to bring some good into this world for all the pain his hands stirred up. Something more than gardening, more than making the kids laugh. Maybe Sam can help him think of something.

When he turns his head to ask, Sam is fast asleep, breathing through his mouth, still a little congested from his breakdown earlier. It won't be the last, he thinks: all of Sam's walls are crumbled down now, after – Luke's certain of it – he's spent the last year steadily trying to build them up, plastering on a strong carefree facade for everyone else, so nobody could see the splintered cracks of him aching deep inside. Just like him to do that, the bloody martyr. Meg next door said Bill did the same thing after he came home, a detached sense of distance he'd worn like a winter coat, a layer of extra padding so it'd hurt less the next time he lost someone close. *My guy's a mess*, Luke had said, sitting beside her on the bench as they watched Bill and his pals stump through the world's slowest game of croquet. *How can I help him get better?*

You? she'd snorted. *Bugger-all. That's on him, sweetie; you can't change another person.* Then she'd softened, laid her wizened hand on his arm. *But you can be his lighthouse, when he's lost adrift in the dark. His rock in the storm. Help him come home. That's what brothers do.*

Troubles, he's come to realise, can't be healed by one thing alone. Grief, hurt, trauma – not anything that wants fixing can be cured in one go. People say it's time, or distance, or love, but you can have all of those in their purest form and still not affect any meaningful change at all, if it isn't the right moment. If the flesh isn't ready. And they're none of them cures, not individually, not altogether as a collective effort. If there's any cure at all, he thinks, it's *living*. Day to day. The humdrum monotony and the fumbling and the moments of blinding joyful light, however absurd – the laundry, the bills, the weeding; children laughing in the meadow, dandelion seeds dancing in the breeze. Pruning the

204

goddamn roses. You put dead things in the compost heap and they eventually come back to life, in another form. Nothing is ever truly destroyed, not forever. They're always reborn soon enough.

He smiles up at the stars. Sam, asleep on his shoulder, doesn't stir.

'Goodnight,' Luke murmurs. 'And thank you, Sergeant Ward.'

REBEL

I skirt around a burst water pipe, hurry across a mangled tramline. The ruins of Berlin sprawl all around me, but my eyes remain upward, inspecting the gap-toothed blue skyline for movement, ears straining for the distant drone of propellers. I crane up on tiptoes, only to get jostled sideways by a woman hurrying past with her head down. Eager to get home, or work, or to her children in the playground. Like life is normal.

Like there isn't a war on.

It sickens me how much my fellow citizens delude themselves. The can rattlers prowling from door to door, their daily exhortations for the

Winter Relief Fund. It's voluntary on paper, but everyone has to chip in. No one dare refuse; we've all heard the stories. Shirkers being betrayed by their whispering neighbours eager to appear good loyal Germans. Losing their jobs. Their family's respect. Denounced and scorned. "People's Community"? People's Snitchers, more like.

The Americans come in the daytime now. No warning. Yesterday afternoon, halfway across Friedrichstrasse, the sirens began their mournful wail. I threw myself to the ground just in time. Pressed my face into the cobbles until I thought my nose would break. When the dust settled and the earth had stopped shuddering, I'd looked up to see a girl impaled on an iron railing, blonde curls hiding her face, her limp fingertips barely kissing the ground. A woman slumped in the rubble, screaming at the bloody stump where her left arm had been.

The sky roars. Louder. Louder. The ground shakes beneath my feet, already afraid of the oncoming storm. I crouch down amid scattered bricks. Can the pilots see me? Are they even now peering down from their pregnant vessels droning among the clouds, their lethal bellyfuls waiting for release? If I stare right back into their goggled eyes, will my image haunt them long after this day, this fateful raid? Will they remember the defiant German woman, whisper her name in hushed reverential tones? Or will they chuckle and snigger over cold beers, tell their grandchildren that she had it coming? Bullseye.

I know I should lie down, hands over my head, but I cannot move. A man yells at me to run, take cover, hide. My body braces, ready for my luck to finally run out, but the sky is a brilliant streak of blue and I've already made my choice: I will stare death boldly in the face, watch the flash of brilliant light, the blaze of my sinews and bones as the searing heat washes over me.

The belly of the plane opens.

I close my eyes.

One . . .

Two . . .

Three . . .

I open my eyes, and can only see white. The scream tears itself from my throat. Something caresses my cheek and I jerk away, shaking my head. What is this? Fragments of the street appear around white corners. I sigh; my breath ripples the paper falling about my face, swirling around my knees. Leaflets – drifting like late snowfall in March – settle on the burst water pipes and shroud the twisted tramline, slowly filling the jagged remains of a clawfoot bathtub. One flutters down right at my feet, like a fallen dove with a broken wing.

I should walk away with my eyes ahead, move on, mimic the hurried shiftiness of others. The brunette in the red dress, carefully picking her way through the rubble. The man with the briefcase striding past. The boy in the Hitler Youth shirt with his catapult poised, the shocking paleness of knobbly knees below his dark lederhosen. I should hurry onward, but the leaflet lures me back. I don't want to read it; I know what it says, believe what it says. I just want to keep it, stow it safely away, treasure those printed promises of a better tomorrow, know that something more exists beyond bombs and brick dust and overflowing cemeteries.

Otto would understand, of course. He waits for me back home, smiling proudly down from the mantelpiece in his smart corporal's uniform. My brave husband snatched from me far too soon. Only his beaming photograph and a typed telegram full of empty meaningless platitudes, now cold ash mouldering in the fireplace. This war is meaningless. Hitler is a murderer, his fanatic followers a pack of liars and cowards who send our husbands, our brothers, our sons off to die.

What do they know of honour? Of duty? Of courage?

We are not fighting the German people, roars the leaflet, *but Hitler's oppressive regime which has enslaved innocent German civilians and robbed them of their freedoms. You are outgunned and outnumbered, but your selfish leaders continue to prolong this bloody conflict for their own cruel ends. Help us end this useless war now. Petition your leaders to surrender and help us bring peace to rebuild a newer, better Germany.*

I gaze at the woman, the man and the boy, then the endless scraps of paper which flutter in the breeze. I stoop low, feigning a wince, curl my fingers and lift up the leaflet. Perhaps anyone looking will assume I injured my side when the plane appeared: my slow cautious movements, my hand rubbing my thigh, the crumpled scrap of treason concealed within.

The price for hoarding enemy leaflets is high – interrogations, cells, the gallows – but I slide the leaflet into my pocket, stand up and walk on, head high. The boy in the Hitler Youth uniform cranes his neck to peer after me, until I turn into a side street and he vanishes from sight. Did he see? Perhaps. Perhaps not.

It's raining again. Grey sheets of rain patter on the roof, rattle against the window. Keeping me in, shutting me out – it's all the same thing.

I can't leave, but I can look about me. I'm glad I chose the top bunk. It's warmer up here and a trickle of condensation runs down the brickwork within tongue's reach. The woman below me hasn't moved in hours.

Emma smiles in the doorway, pale and beloved, her sightless blue-grey eyes steady and reassuring. Too precious to me now and the last thing I'll let slip from me if I die here. Her hands are the ones I know most, more than my own. How many hours have I have traced the lines on her dry wizened palm, stroked her dry papery cheek?

Of course the boy saw me. Of course. He'd seen me pocket the fallen leaflet and scuttled

211

along to his next junior meeting, greedy for praise. Before long came the fateful knock just after midnight. Two leather-coated Gestapo awaited me outside. What else could I do?

At least Mother is safe.

From her bunk below, Ruth whispers that they are coming. The guards here keep a casual watch, some drunk and violent. Reprisals come fast, deadly and unquestioned. I haven't seen Clara ever since yesterday when they dragged her away. She'd spoken of her nineteenth birthday at the café, dancing to her sister's violin, her laughter as Papa slipping her lemonade and chocolates under the counter. She made light of the cold dampness of our cell, of the stinking reek of the slop bucket.

She'd pushed her last bread crust into my hands as they kicked open the door and marched inside, more life for me in the final precious minutes of hers. I wanted to save it, treasure it in memory of her, but I still gobbled it all up. It did not nourish me.

More shouting outside, the rattle of chains, the sharp crack of gunshots. Lorries roar. The air smells burnt. Emma is here more than ever. She makes me happy. She would cheer Ruth up too,

I'm sure, but whenever I ask her to say hello she won't. She just weeps in frustration, curled up on her cot below. 'Who are you talking to?' she sobs, waving a hand at the thick iron door. 'There's nobody there.'

She's taken next morning. I can't even say goodbye.

The interrogator's hair is thinning. He's combed it back and darkened it with oil, but he isn't fooling anyone.

The leaflet lies between us like a shameful naked sore, like a poison stain on the tabletop. The only contraband they needed to haul me in here, charge me, sentence me to death. He peers at me over his owlish spectacles. 'You know the penalty for harbouring treasonous lies.'

I glower back at him, arms folded. Of course I do. The shadow of the guillotine looms over us all here in Plötzensee. For me it's a hanging, one final cruel pettiness by the sneering judge. At least it'll be quick. I hope.

He removes his glasses and cleans them. Flashes me a rueful smile. 'Who else assisted you in this? Please understand . . . you need to tell me because I *will* be asked, and I *have* to answer my superiors.'

I shake my head and stare back, tightlipped. No one else is guilty of my crimes.

'Do you have any final requests?'

I name them. To his credit, he doesn't smirk, or snigger, or gloat. He simply turns to the grey-coated sentry at the doorway and orders: 'Make sure she's brought here safe and sound. If anything untoward should happen to her, you'll answer to me.' The sentry clicks his heels and marches out the door.

All this fuss for one fallen leaflet? Chains clink as I raise a manacled hand to hide my smirk.

Good thing they never found the hidden stash concealed behind the toilet.

Sunlight slices through the window bars, splashing over your face. I will carry this piecemeal image – eyes scrunched shut, your late father's nose, pink lips suckling – with me to the hangman's noose.

Not long left, *Liebling*. Each blessed moment is precious. You've kept me alive longer than I ever hoped. Pregnancy and mother's milk count for something in these dark times. Yes, I've done my part fattening you up for the Reich. Your rosy cheeks. Your healthy limbs. But another baby for the Führer, you are not. Never will be. I've cradled you close, whispered words you'll never remember. Be more. Resist. In darkness and dampness I've told you of those still out there, fighting the good fight. I've spoken in code, soothed you in Russian. I've armed you as if you were a fresh-faced eighteen-year-old recruit for the cause, not a helpless infant about to be handed off to a life extending well beyond mine.

I pace around the cell, rocking you. Sometimes I count, singing each step into a makeshift rolling lullaby you might someday remember. Perhaps on a rainy Thursday a window cleaner will pass humming a note, and you'll feel the walls close in around you, see how the light splinters through the window glass, smell my milky odour, hear my crooning voice. Broken. Bloody. Unbowed.

A rat scurries out of the darkness; it stops amid the filthy floor and glares up as if it were my landlord and I owe it rent. I want to stamp my feet, chase it off, but instead I turn my back and focus on your whimpers. I kiss your forehead. Once. Twice. Thrice. On and on. A kiss for every birthday I'll miss. A kiss for every bruised knee and skinned elbow I won't soothe. For every question that will hang unanswered over the dining table until the time's right and your grandmother spills forth what she remembers.

I shift you so your head rests beneath my chin, your fists clenched against my chest. Your lips bubble and slurp, a sweet *shik-shik* suckle of air as I curl around you, savouring your butterscotch scent. You pause to gape a greedy smile, swallowing the night; you are ready for this life. I listen to your deep drowsy breath, savour the dry roughness of your cradle cap against my skin. Your grandmother has a remedy for that. She'll have a remedy for everything, except my absence. You will climb into her arms, grow up to her shoulders, cry in her lap.

I sway to the sounds of prison: my next-door inmate coughing, dirty feet shuffling across cold floors, the thud of metal on metal, the shrill demands of the women who've yet to accept their sentences. I have accepted mine. I know pleading with a madman is futile. I could wail and bang my fists against the bars, but that would mean putting you down and I won't do that, not until they prise you from my white-knuckled

216

fingers.

I lean forward to whisper into your mouth, for you to taste my final parting words: you were, are, will be loved. Always. You'll grow up beautiful, I'll always be with you. I'll see you again one day . . .

Not long now. I can hear the crunch of heels on concrete, the steady gait of someone with a grim purpose. The harsh rattle of keys. I square my shoulders and breathe out, for I will not go gentle into that long night. I will meet my end proudly, head high and heart singing. For you.

I wonder how you'll think of me, for you won't remember me but will know I existed: every child has a mother, after all. I hope when you hear my story that you're in a better time. A time of peace and plenty. I hope you bombard your grandmother with questions beyond the colour of my eyes and my favourite pair of shoes. She'll tell you all that, but you must ask her why I'm not there. Don't accept that I died in childbirth or during a bombing raid. Don't accept that I was caught up with the wrong people, that I went against the Führer and got what I deserved, that the leaflets I dropped spewed lies and dissent. The world around you is a lie, and if by the time you've grown taller than your grandmother this country is still red, white, and black, you must find your people, our people, and do what I did. Rise up. Resist.

Pray for your sins, the prison chaplain had urged me.

Instead I prayed for you, rejoicing in the sin that birthed you. I prayed that you grow strong, prayed that no one ever steers you away from your loved ones, and I prayed that you will grow up in a new world. A new age of peace and freedom. A better future that I helped forge, even with my single flickering spark.

That's the beauty of a single candle, my darling, even a shrunken melted stub like mine. The darkness is brutal, the darkness is powerful, and it swallows all beneath it, but in that strength lies its greatest weakness: one lone guttering candle is enough to hold it back. One single spark of resistance, and it shrinks back against the wall, cringing from the light.

Truth and love will always win. There have been tyrants and murderers throughout history, and for a time they seemed invincible. Unbeatable. Eternal. But the cracks will always appear, and in the end they always fall. They always have.

For too long have we cowered in the shadow of the swastika, been crushed beneath the jackboot of tyranny. A million voices across Europe now roaring aloud with one mighty voice: *No more.*

Be proud of the resistance thrumming through your bloodline. But take extra care of your life. Always look twice, then twice again. Take detours. Cross busy streets. Never pause. Never look back.

Metal screeches on metal. The warden standing on the threshold inclines her head. Extends her arms. You'll leave first. I lift you so we're face to face, swaddle you tight so you won't feel the cold. Your eyelids droop, you gurgle in my arms. I kiss the crinkle between your eyebrows, breathe in your precious lingering scent. Your weight slips from my hands into a stranger's unfamiliar arms, and you cry.

You will bawl your way out of this place into the daylight. Your grandmother will shush you on the walk to the U-Bahn, kiss your forehead on the train to Alexanderplatz, sing a lullaby as she carries you upstairs to her apartment on Torstrasse, with its peeling wallpaper and the lingering smell of mildew. And then you will quieten into slumber and your life will go on. With my everlasting love. I will always be with you, like the unseen nightingale: out of sight but singing, my darling, out of sight but singing.

Hope is more than just a candle.

Hope can ignite the stars.

I clench my fists, close my eyes to your tear-stained cheeks, and turn away. The warden mutters as she struggles to calm your flailing limbs. I smile despite the sudden chill of loneliness. In the precious hours left before the gallows, before my final long walk down these cold stone corridors, I will always remember you as rebellious.

It runs in the family, I guess.

About the Author

Half Welsh, half Brummie, and terrible at both accents, Tom Burton has lived in Nigeria, Oman and the Netherlands. He currently lives and writes with his family in Devon, his imagination nourished by the magic of dark chocolate and Yorkshire Tea.

His short stories have featured in numerous online journals including *Spillwords Press*, *Literally Stories*, *Dreaming in Fiction* and *Whatever Keeps the Lights On*.

Pocketful of Time is his second self-published collection of short stories, after *Wildlands* (2020). Visit his website to find out more:

www.slumdogsoldier.wordpress.com

Printed in Great Britain
by Amazon

70900064R00135